BEYOND THE WALL

A Novel

L.J. Vanterra

Beyond the Wall

Tellwell Talent
www.tellwell.ca

ISBN
978-1-998454-88-4 (Paperback)

Just living is not enough... one must have sunshine, freedom, and a little flower.

Hans Christian Andersen

There is freedom waiting for you,
On the breezes of the sky,
And you ask "What if I fall?"
Oh but my darling,
What if you fly?

Erin Hanson

CHAPTER 1

The door opened just wide enough for a human to be pushed through it. With a clank, the door slammed shut behind her, sealing the new arrival's fate. *The compound is already crowded*, thought Adnil. An additional person in their living quarters would make it even tighter.

Adnil felt the walls closing in and went outside into the yard to seek more space. She paced the well-worn dirt path that ran parallel to the high wall bordering the yard. Two women were crouched in their usual place near the centre of the square playing a competitive game involving tossing stones at a target. It was neither complicated nor exciting, but it helped pass the time. They were known as Valda and Dawn, but they did not always have those names. Women arrived at this compound nameless, labelled only with a unique identifier coded into a band worn around the left wrist.

"Come and join us," Valda hollered. They had invited Adnil to participate in their game before but she always politely declined. She wasn't much of a joiner. She was not fond of the idle chit-chat that often accompanied playing games, finding the conversation laborious and pointless. "No thanks, not today," Adnil replied, knowing that her response would likely be the same another day.

Adnil shivered and felt the muscles in her neck tighten. The cool wind left goosebumps on her exposed tan calves, making her wish her tunic went to her ankles rather than ending just below the knees. She paced faster, hoping it would heat her up, but finally went indoors where it was warmer—although only slightly. The bunks were filled with women, most sleeping, a few with eyes wide open staring straight ahead at nothing. Adnil walked down one of the many narrow aisles between the rows of bunks stacked three high and climbed up to her top one. Although she claimed it as her bunk, it had never actually been assigned to her. However, it was the one she had slept in since arriving at the compound. Stretching out on her back, Adnil closed her eyes so she did not have to look at the ceiling, an arm's length from her eyes. Pulling the thin blanket tightly around her neck, she lay still, listening to the chorus of snores and whistling breaths emanating from her bunkmates. She tried to pick out a rhythmic pattern in the cacophony of sounds. The combination of nasal whispers, heavy hums, soft purrs, and the occasional stuttering snort provided an eclectic mix of percussive tones; a peculiar symphony only an imaginative mind could enjoy. The meditative escape relaxed Adnil and the muscles in her stiff neck began to melt like soft snow on a warm spring day.

The peaceful moment was shattered when the locked door joining their quarters to the medical room burst open. Two "commanders" dressed in blue jumpsuits bounded in. Adnil tensed as they began searching the compound, big yellow alien eyes rapidly scanning every area. Sleeping pads were tossed off bunks as they inspected under each one.

What are they looking for? thought Adnil as she quickly climbed down from her bunk and moved to the other side of the room. Most had managed to back away from the tall, menacing figures, trying to stay clear of the action. The few still in their bunks, frozen with fear, were grabbed by the arms and roughly tossed aside.

"NuqZaq? wInIZla Xbe'chugh?" one of the tall aliens shouted, making Adnil jump.

You'd think that being held captive by these aliens my whole life, I would have picked up a bit of their language, thought Adnil. However, she had never put any effort into that area. Besides, the commanders seldom spoke to each other in the presence of the women.

"NuqZaq? wInIZla Xbe'chugh?" they shouted louder.

Hearing the commotion, Valda and Dawn came in from the yard and stood in the doorway, observing the turbulent inspection. Finally, the commanders left, having found nothing. They swiped their wristbands across a scanner to exit, and left the women in the locked compound behind them.

"What do you think the yellow-eyed monsters were looking for?" asked one of the women when they were gone.

Adnil noticed Valda and Dawn whispering to each other, smiling with satisfaction. "What secrets are you hiding? What were they looking for?" Adnil's brown eyes narrowed into a glare.

"We're working on something. The less you know for now, the better," Valda replied.

"You are going to get us all in a real mess," said Adnil.

"Mess? Our lives are already a mess," said Dawn. "We're working on a plan to get us *out* of this mess. One day, you'll see."

Adnil rubbed her stiff neck. She picked up sleeping pads from the dirty floor and placed them back on the bunks before climbing back up to her bunk and closing her eyes. *What were they looking for?* She detested them and hated the fact that they controlled her and all those around her. She hated her life in the compound. She wished she had been born in an era when humans were free. Everyone referred to that glorious time as BC: before colonization. Unfortunately, while Earthlings were exploring Mars, and fighting amongst themselves about rights and jurisdiction on the red planet, inhabitants of a lesser-known planet had their eyes fixed on Earth.

As Adnil lay in her bunk, she wondered what her life would have been like if the commanders—Xplerians—had not invaded the planet. Born in captivity, this was the only world she knew: living like a farm animal in servitude to another species, hoping and dreaming of things unknown, but longed for still. Deep in thought, she dozed off. Waking sometime later with her nostrils feeling stuffed up and dry, she headed to the yard for some fresh air.

Adnil looked upward, wishing a strong wind could scoop her up and carry her away. In her periphery, she spotted a feral cat, its orange fur standing out in contrast to the drab roof it was walking on. With its head hung low, and its tail straight out, the feline exhibited a confident stride. Adnil admired its agility as each step was taken with precision and full control. Watching the cat's balancing act brought some pleasure to her dull days. However, their relationship was far from symbiotic, as the cat never seemed to notice her while flaunting its freedom with rooftop theatrics. Sometimes the cat walked along the top of the wall, but it was never in the actual yard. It too must know that once in the compound yard, there was no way of getting out.

Adnil closed her eyes and inhaled deeply, appreciating the fresh air as it re-energized her spirit. When she opened her eyes, the cat was gone. Adnil's gaze descended from the rooftop to the images carved on the face of the wall. The walls designed to keep her and the others confined doubled as a gallery exhibiting images etched by its occupants. The wall's smooth surface made it an ideal canvas, while stones found on the ground served as carving tools. Some images revealed anger, some hope, while others were simple doodles scratched out in a moment of boredom. Adnil smiled as she looked at an enormous caricature of a commander: a tall stick-like body with an oversized head and large eyes. Divots dotted the caricature's head—marks left by those who cathartically threw stones at it. Ignoring the chill, Adnil picked up a rock and drew a bird on the wall. She envied the freedom birds had. They were always on the move. Much time was spent watching little ones darting about, briefly landing on the wall or in the yard before taking off again. Occasionally, as the warm season faded, groups of larger birds could be seen collaboratively journeying across the sky in a V formation.

A rumbling noise from above caught Adnil's attention. Looking up, she saw an airplane moving across the sky, like a spider making a long journey across a wall. She had been told by "originals"—those who had lived in the outside world before colonization—that airplanes were vessels designed to transport large numbers of beings or cargo from one point on the planet to another, but to her it was just a speck moving across the sky. Adnil had a hard time imagining how this tiny speck could carry anything, or how it could stay suspended without falling out of the sky. *Does it have wings like a bird that enable it to fly?* The outside world was a mystery to her. Not having lived in it herself, the knowledge shared by the originals was the only source of information she had about it.

Adnil watched the airplane move across the sky until it disappeared, blocked by the high wall. She lingered in the yard, preferring the quietness it offered at the moment, although the one-size-fits-all green tunic did not sufficiently protect her from the chilly air. She pulled the blanket she had draped over her shoulders more tightly around her. The days were getting shorter and cooler; it would be a long time before the air would be warm enough to walk around without wrapping oneself in blankets.

Adnil's stomach growled as the sun dropped below the top of the wall. The sky was her timepiece. The celestial bodies and the change in seasons were the few ways to tell that time was passing. Otherwise one might think time stood still. Each day in Adnil's regimented life was exactly the same. There was nothing new to look forward to, no goals to set, nothing to achieve, no significant days, no dreams to fulfil, and no need for ambition.

Adnil's breasts started to tingle as she waited for the bell, calling the women to the evening ritual. When it finally sounded, she and the rest of the women trooped to their stations. She sat on the hard stool, opened the front of her tunic, and pulled the two cup-like funnels towards her. She attached one to each breast, then waved her wristband over the sensor. A clamp extended and held her left hand in position. As her milk let down, and was pulled through the funnels into the hoses hanging from the ceiling, it triggered the release of food into the bowl in front of her. She might loathe the ritual, but it was the only way to get fed in the compound. Adnil breathed in the aroma and picked up some of the thick, pureed mush with her free right hand. The soft food felt good on her tongue. It had an earthy, savoury flavour that she found satisfying. As the pumps continued to extract milk, Adnil finished her meal.

CHAPTER 2

The sound of the bell hit Adnil's eardrums like thunder on a stormy night. *Ugh! The last thing I want to do in the dead of night is to leave my bunk.* She felt the bunk posts sway as others vacated the bunks below her and knew she should follow suit. In defiance, her body's paralysis tried to convince her to drift back into dreamland, a somnolent state, away from her cruel world.

A flicker of focus brought Adnil back to ugly reality, but her languid limbs still refused to be lifted from the mattress. It was tempting to skip the midnight milking session, but she knew she would regret it if she did. Her stomach was rumbling now, and she would be even hungrier in the morning if she did not get her body out of the bunk and to a station. The small portions dispensed at each of the four milking sessions were part of their overall volume of food. Women who regularly skipped the midnight milking withered away, like a parched plant during a drought, and were prematurely removed from the compound.

Adnil finally left her bunk and shuffled over to the milk stations. She yawned as she sat on one of the last empty stools and slowly reached for the funnel cups. Not everyone had a problem waking up in the middle of the night. In fact, some had told her they automatically woke up, right before the bell.

Adnil moved food to her mouth almost without thinking. Through sleepy eyes, she could see Valda and Dawn at nearby stations whispering to each other. They appeared wide awake, not at all like they had just been woken from a deep slumber by an irritating bell.

With the ritual over, Adnil crawled back into her bunk and closed her eyes. This was her favourite time, with nothing separating them and the morning light except more sleep and a chance to dream, to fantasize about a better life. Adnil lay still, waiting to escape to her dreams, but sleep refused to return, robbing her of the retreat. She took in a deep breath, hoping it would relax her. Musty air filled her nostrils, making its way down into her lungs. Trying to ignore it, she rolled over onto her side, pulling the blanket up over her head. She visualized herself lying on a soft cloud, but her hip digging into the thin mattress was determined to tell its own story. Rolling to her back again, she took in another deep breath. The stench was still there. Her patience finally ran out and she climbed down from her bunk and bolted to the yard.

Adnil pulled the blanket higher to keep the cool wind off her neck and looked into the dark, foreboding sky. Clouds obscured the stars normally visible, and the moon too was temporarily hidden from view. She peered deeply into the silent darkness, missing the comfort normally provided by her celestial acquaintances.

Something rustled in the far corner of the yard, breaking the solemn silence. Adnil's body stiffened as her eyes shifted in the direction of the potential threat. She prayed that it was simply nocturnal rodents exploring in the safety of the darkness. She swallowed hard as the rustling grew louder and sounded less like mice playing in the dirt. The passing clouds thinned, allowing the moon to shed filtered light into the yard. Adnil could make out two silhouettes, bent over, looking at the ground. She watched as they stood erect and was relieved that they were not tall enough to be commanders. The moonlight reflected off several shiny objects laid out on the ground at their feet. As they arranged the objects, Adnil recognized the familiar posture of Valda and Dawn. *What are they doing out here?* The shiny objects were starting to look familiar too. She watched as Dawn gathered tools used by the commanders to prod, poke, and inject, and wrapped them up in a blanket. Adnil retreated to her bunk before she could be seen.

CHAPTER 3

Adnil's stomach growled as she lay in her bunk waiting for the bell to summon them to the morning milking session. The small, dirty window overlooking the yard provided no indication of day or night in this season of dark mornings. The bell finally rang, bringing both angst and relief to Adnil's weary soul. Seeing long line-ups at the two toilets, Adnil took a drink from the water fountain and went straight to a milking station. She could use the toilet later while waiting for the daily education session to start.

Joy, who was leading today's education session, centred herself between the rows of milking stations so she could be heard by everyone, and seen by most. With limited space, most things took place in the same area: they'd defecate openly in the same place they ate their food and had their breasts pumped. Privacy was a privilege that was non-existent. The bunks were separated from the milking area, although the adjoining room was still not private due to the open-concept design of the compound. Those who chose not to stay for the education class retreated to the yard if the weather was tolerable, or to their bunk, to try to tune out the unsolicited sound.

Joy stood on a crate once left behind by a commander after a task. The added height allowed her to make a better visual connection with the group, but more importantly, allowed her to keep an eye on the door, ready to abandon the session should a commander enter. Joy pulled the matted sandy-blond hair away from her face before she spoke. Like a gifted orator, her voice rose with eloquence, connecting with the audience.

"I welcome you to today's education session and remind you why we participate in this important practice." Joy opened with this statement every time, and Adnil had the introduction that followed embedded in her brain.

"We are a people colonized by an alien species who have enslaved the human race," Joy continued. "Our bondage keeps us cut off from the outside world, and without stimulation, our minds will deteriorate. We must keep our brains active, and commit to retaining the knowledge of the outside world, at least what we had before we were cut off from it."

Although Joy repeated this preamble before every session, she said it with the same fervour each time, like she was announcing it to a new audience.

"You don't need a brain to supply milk," Aaron often retorted, not alone in wondering what the point was of keeping their brains active. Aaron claimed her motivation for attending the sessions was simply to pass the time and find some relief from boredom. "I'm not here to increase brain cells," she regularly declared. Yet she never missed a session, standing tall on the periphery, twirling her long, black, matted hair, not wanting to be part of the group, yet subconsciously hungry for intellectual stimulation.

"One day our people will be free again," Joy professed, with raised eyebrows, looking sincere and bright-eyed for the future.

"I believe the practice of holding human women captive as milk producers will eventually be discontinued by the Xplerians."

Adnil was skeptical. She wanted to believe Joy, but saw no signs that freedom was on the horizon.

#

"Some ant species herd aphids and take their milk," Joy said to Adnil one night in the yard. Joy was full of fun facts, which she gladly shared if she felt she was in the company of a receptive listener. "In extreme cases, ants clip off the wings of their domesticated aphids to prevent them from flying away when they mature."

Adnil frowned at the description of the abuse.

"However, there have been many other examples in history where species have evolved, modifying their diet, and no longer exploiting other beings for food," Joy continued. "Humans, for example."

"What?" Adnil was not sure if she had heard correctly.

"Humans were once guilty of enslaving other animals to exploit them for their milk."

"Really!?"

"Ironically, we despise the commanders for what they do to us, but our ancestors did the same thing." Joy shook her head, as if the hypocrisy had just occurred to her.

"I wish I wasn't born a milker." Adnil looked down despondently.

"One isn't born a milker, one becomes one," said Joy. "The role is assigned to you after you enter the world, based on species, gender, and the era you happen to be born into."

"Three for three, I guess we were unlucky."

Sometimes Adnil got a taste of freedom in her dreams, when her consciousness retreated, unaware that she was a milker, and she was wild and free. Not defined by others, she flew like a bird just below the clouds. With hollow bones, she could soar with ease, inspecting the world below through eagle eyes. Although a fantasy, it was the only time she really felt like herself.

Differing opinions about what would give rise to their freedom existed among the inhabitants of the compound. Some thought they might be set free if the Xplerians were overtaken by a more dominant species who had no desire for human milk. Others agreed with Joy that the Xplerians' evolving morality would end the practice of enslavement.

"You're living in a dream world," said Valda. "Your idealistic thoughts about Xplerians coming to some kind of enlightenment and ending milking are absurd. We'll be free again one day, but it won't be because the yellow-eyed monsters suddenly gain morals."

Although Valda saw value in the education sessions, she disapproved when Joy included a righteous rant about Xplerians' future enlightenment and repentance.

"Might is right," Valda would counter. "That's the only reason we are in this compound. That is how nature works. We are part of the food chain. If things were different, it might be humans eating spiced Xplerian balls every night for dinner."

Regardless of what would bring it about, many felt future freedom was realistic. Even if the possibility was slim, hope was all they had to keep them going. If liberation took place during their lifetime and they were not prepared to cope in the outside world, their chances of surviving would be decreased. Without real-time access to information about the outside world, the milkers were reliant on knowledge retained by the originals who had been captured when the Xplerians colonized Earth. Like sponges, they absorbed facts about a world they longed to enter.

#

Pre-colonization, Joy never imagined a time when she couldn't access information with the touch of her fingers or the sound of her voice. Her father had been thrilled when she followed in her late mother's footsteps and decided to specialize in space engineering. He hadn't said so, not wanting to bias her decision, but she could tell in his eyes when she revealed her choice that it pleased him. In grad school, she had devoured new knowledge like a curious explorer, but here in the compound, her library of information was limited to what her brain had retained. Although not an expert in everything, she had enough basic information to provide a broad overview of most subjects.

Today they were learning about the different species that inhabit Earth. Joy sometimes co-taught with a younger original when it came to biology, since it was really Robin's forte. Robin had studied biology and got through one year of medical school before Earth was colonized. The teachers shared that they belong to a species called *Homo sapiens* or humans, which was one species among many. The number of unique species had been declining as Earth became less hospitable due to overcrowding and decreased species-specific habitat. Several animals had been wiped out before Earth's colonization, as well as many insect, bird, and aquatic species. In contrast, populations of *tiny* organisms such as viruses and bacteria had thrived, the pernicious ones wreaking havoc on the lives of the larger hosts they invaded.

"Why did they choose humans to invade?" said Adnil.

"It wasn't just humans, but viruses and bacteria need a host species that is reliable long term. While many other species were facing population decline, humans were experiencing a population explosion—making them the best long-term host. So, the germs moved in like uninvited guests, some cohabitating agreeably, while others knocked the human population down a few notches."

"Wait a minute … a big creature was defenceless against a tiny thing ya can't even see?" said Aaron.

"Size does not always equate power," said Joy.

"But Xplerians are taller than us, and they overpowered us," said Adnil.

"Having superior abilities to adapt and survive is what ultimately makes a life form more powerful," said Joy. "Viruses were able to adapt to humans. It's similar to how intelligence involves observing and learning before acting. Xplerians, for example, learned about human behaviour patterns and used it to their advantage."

"What? Are you saying that the commanders are … more intelligent than us?" asked Aaron, still fixated on being labelled inferior.

"In some aspects, yes."

"I'm looking forward to the day when I prove you wrong," said Valda with a confident smile.

"Humans have a history of claiming to be the most intelligent species, but many non-humans have disproved that theory," said Joy. "Even creatures without brains have outsmarted us and taken advantage of humans many times."

"Didn't humans try to fight back against the viruses?" asked Aaron.

"When harmful ones invade, the human body tries to kill them or expel them from within, but often with little success," said Joy.

"Seems kinda pointless, all this fighting between species," said Adnil. "Can't creatures figure it out and just learn to live together?"

"Some species do have that figured out," said Joy. "They tolerate each other and, in some cases, mutually benefit each other. Symbiosis is one expression of intelligent life."

Joy brought the focus back to an overview of mammals. Adnil had heard this part before, but found it just as interesting each time she heard it.

"Mammals have hair, but unlike humans, the hair on some mammals covers their entire body," continued Joy.

Adnil fancied the concept of hair covering the entire body and imagined how much warmer it must feel, especially now during the cold season. She wouldn't get chilled at night for lack of sufficient blankets.

"Some mammals walk on two legs just like us, but there are many who walk on four," Joy further explained.

"Okay, that explains why we're the ones in this hole. With their advantage, the four-legged creatures could run frickin circles around the yellow-eyed monsters," said Valda, causing a roar of laughter.

In subsequent sessions, they learned about other animals such as fish, birds, reptiles, amphibians, and insects, and then switched to learning about their captors.

"Why would we want to know anything about the yellow-eyed monsters?" asked a recent arrival, narrowing her eyes.

"One must study their enemy," said Joy. "If you don't understand how you became enslaved in the first place, you won't recognize the opportunity to change your situation when it arises."

Joy proceeded to give a brief historical review, mostly for the benefit of those who recently arrived at the compound. "We had no knowledge of Xplerians before colonization. Their invasion caught us off guard." She remembered how shocked she had been when she was captured. Having just left a campus pub where she had been celebrating with friends, she was on her way home to have dinner with her father and brother. She was grabbed as she was walking through the school gardens and thrown into the back of a white vehicle.

"Humans were focussed on setting up a colony on Mars," Joy explained. "They were tasked with extracting resources and transporting them to Earth in a space elevator. Meanwhile, aliens from a Super-Earth planet called Xpleria had developed an advanced civilization capable of interstellar spaceflight. They too left their home planet in search of new worlds and resources. Eventually, the Xplerians launched a powerful rocket and made first contact, catching humans off guard. That is when everything changed. The global invasion occurred on all continents simultaneously, a well-laid-out plan. Earth, once dominated by humans, was rapidly overtaken by the Xplerians."

"Mars? Is that the red planet?" piped up Aaron, recalling a past lesson. "Why is it red?"

"It's the iron oxide soil that gives Mars its red colour," answered Joy, happy to have an inquisitive student. "Human astronomers in Egypt first observed the planet Mars. Babylonian astronomers marked its course through the night sky to track the passage of time. But it was not until 1610 when Galileo witnessed Mars through a telescope that Mars was revealed as a whole other world. In Babylonian astronomy, Mars was named after Nergel, the deity of fire, war, and destruction. In Chinese and Japanese texts, the planet was known as the fire star."

The questions from the younger women popped up like hailstones bouncing off the ground. "What does Babylonian mean?" "What is a telescope?" "What's fire?" "What is war?" "What is text?" *There is lots to teach and lots to learn,* thought Joy.

Although the endless questions took the conversation off-topic and down other tangents, Joy did not mind. The curiosity that spurred those questions was a good sign that the young women were eager to learn about the outside world and adept at absorbing knowledge. However, she eventually brought the conversation back to the topic of the Xplerians.

"Although the commanders and their kind originate from another planet, they resemble us more than some mammals from Earth," said Joy. "They have a lot of human-like features. Like us, they walk upright on two legs. Their planet of origin has a similar atmosphere to Earth, which is why they can cope so well here. Earth's atmosphere contains about seventy-eight percent nitrogen and twenty-one percent oxygen, with trace amounts of other gases. Xpleria's atmosphere is similar enough that they can breathe Earth's air unassisted."

"Well isn't it nice that the yellow-eyed monsters felt so much at home after arriving uninvited," said Dawn sarcastically.

"It is likely that the aliens had been studying humans long before they arrived here," continued Joy. "It appeared they arrived with a mission, already familiar with the planet, and with a plan in hand. It did not take them long to round us up."

"So, the intruders were comfortable here, liked what they saw, and just took over? That isn't right!" said Aaron.

"Might is right," muttered Valda, shaking her head as she abandoned the session and headed for the yard.

"Our time is coming," stated Dawn, as she followed Valda out the door.

#

Adnil looked up at the night sky thinking about Joy's lesson earlier that day. She watched her warm breath as it dissipated into the cold air. Adnil found it fascinating to hear stories about other planets. The compound walls kept them totally cut off from the outside world, yet ironically, from the yard, they were able to look straight up to the sky and see faraway places. On clear nights the sky offered Adnil an artistic display of fascinating celestial objects to view: stars, constellations, bright planets, and the ever-changing moon. She wondered how many other milkers were staring up at the sky at this very moment. *Are there milkers trapped within walled yards all over the world just like me? Or is it more large-scale than that? Are milkers trapped within walled yards on planets throughout the universe? Are they looking in my direction and seeing the planet Earth in their night sky?*

"Hello, is there anybody out there?" she said out loud.

"It's a beautiful clear sky tonight," said Joy as she walked up behind Adnil. "And look, you can see Venus."

"Where? Show me!"

Joy placed her arms on Adnil's shoulders and positioned her in the right direction, then pointed. "Venus is the brightest object in the sky after the sun and the moon."

"Do you think humans or species from other planets have gone to Venus?" asked Adnil.

"It's hard to say, but likely not," replied Joy. "At the time of Earth's colonization, humans were putting all their effort into exploring Mars. Although harsh, the atmosphere on the surface of Mars is more hospitable than that of other nearby planets. Venus, for example, is considered one of the hottest places in the solar system. Despite the somewhat harsh surface on Mars, humans found a way of adapting."

"How did they cope if it was so harsh?" Adnil shivered.

"Actually, the first surface explorations were done with robots," said Joy. "But with the creation of specially designed space suits to block radiation and provide warmth, humans were able to join the robots on the planet's surface. Then, with the introduction of terraforming, the temperature on Mars warmed up a bit, making it somewhat more hospitable to humans. Instead of the heavy-duty space suits, they could wear lighter outfits."

"I wonder what it must have felt like for the first humans who lived on Mars," said Adnil. "Going to an unknown world must have been a bit scary."

"Yes, but also thrilling." Joy remembered how excited she had been as a fresh graduate from the space engineering program. She had applied for a space mission and was waiting to hear whether she would be accepted. "We might get to experience the excitement of going to an unknown world one day."

"Did humans live together in communities on Mars, or did they spread out?" asked Adnil.

"They lived together. The first human-built colonies on Mars were located at the poles, where they found ice deposits." Joy was always happy to oblige an inquisitive listener. "The settlers extracted some of the ice and turned it into liquid water. They also used resources on Mars to create glass and brick buildings for their colony."

Adnil savoured the moment she was having with Joy as they looked up at the night sky. They were alone in the yard, which was rare considering they lived in tight quarters with a lot of people. This moment was special to Adnil. She looked up to Joy, admiring the way she was able to retain information and pass the oral history along to others. She also admired the positive manner and sense of hope Joy exuded, particularly about being released one day. Adnil appreciated Joy's dedication to preparing the women for such a day. In turn, Joy delighted in watching the amazement on Adnil's young face as she looked up at Venus, absorbing the beauty and wonder of it all.

"You would make a great teacher, Adnil."

"Me? But I can't. I haven't lived in the outside world."

"True, but you have a zest for knowledge and a bank of information from listening to all my lessons over the years."

Adnil looked awkwardly at the ground, but internally, the compliment pleased her. She admired Joy and was elated that Joy thought she would make a good teacher one day.

"I'm too young. There are several that have been listening to education sessions a lot longer than I have."

"Yes, but it takes more than that to be a good teacher," said Joy. "We need you, Adnil. You have a calm manner and an appreciation for learning. Besides, I won't be around forever and there aren't many originals left."

Adnil's heart dropped at the comment, but their attention was quickly diverted by lively singing and rhythmic hand-clapping coming from inside the compound.

> In my dreams, we are free,
> Flying together, you and me.
> In my dreams, we are free,
> Exploring like a bumblebee.
>
> Yeh, yeh, yeh, we are free,
> Yeh, yeh, yeh, we are free.
> Nobody is caging me,
> Cuz we have found our liberty.
>
> In my dreams, we are free,
> Walking together, you and me.
> In my dreams, we are free,
> Strolling by the deep blue sea.
>
> Yeh, yeh, yeh, I am free.
> Yeh, yeh, yeh, I am free.
> Nobody is caging me,
> Cuz we have found our liberty.

Joy and Adnil knew the words to this familiar song and smiled as they heard the promising lyrics and the exuberance with which it was being sung. Valda and Dawn added an amusing verse.

> In my dreams, I am free
> And the commander is serving me.
> In my dreams, I am free.
> And it is obeying me.

Laughter followed, encouraging Valda and Dawn to continue with the chorus.

> Yeh, yeh, yeh, I am free.
> Yeh, yeh, yeh, I am free.
> In my dreams, I am free,
> And the commander is serving me.

The women had a vast library of songs, some historical ones created before colonization, others newer, created in captivity. Unlike the education sessions, the singing sessions were not scheduled, but erupted spontaneously most evenings. It was when the women were most relaxed and hopeful for a better day ahead.

Moved by the pull of the music, Joy and Adnil smiled at each other and walked arm in arm to join the frivolity.

CHAPTER 4

Joy held tears back as she watched another original being removed from the compound. Her heart grieved, knowing the chances of not returning were high for a milker of a certain age. Joy couldn't know for sure what happened when they were removed, but her gut told her it was likely the end for them. Losing an original was tough on the remaining ones. The bond between originals was strong due to their shared experience, and it only grew stronger as their numbers shrank. Having lived in the outside world, they received respect from the younger milkers, who entrusted them with the honourable role of knowledge keepers. But membership in this privileged group came with a cost—the certainty that they faced the earliest elimination.

"Now there are just two of us," said Robin.

"Yes," Joy said quietly as she stared down at the ground in deep thought.

The responsibility of teaching weighed heavily on Joy. She knew that trained non-originals would eventually have to take over leading the education sessions, although she hoped they would be freed before it came to that. For now, the job fell on her shoulders with occasional help from Robin.

"I can lead more sessions if you like, Joy. I'd like to share the load. Besides…"

"Besides what?"

"Nothing. It's just that you have a lot on your plate, and … I am willing to teach more than I am now."

An awkward silence hung in the air as Robin waited for a response.

"You're probably right, Robin. I could use more help. After all, you have a year of medical school under your belt so you could take over the sessions on biology." Then she quickly added with a firm voice, "But you know how I feel about what to reveal."

"But isn't it wrong to hold back information?" said Robin.

"Under different circumstances, I would agree, Robin. But revealing every unpleasant fact would just add more pain to their miserable lives. Truth is virtuous, but sometimes there is a cost to revealing unnecessary detail. Right now, I'm more concerned about their mental well-being."

"You know I respect your opinion, Joy, so I promise to show restraint and tone down the content."

Joy valued honesty. She would never lie to the women if asked a direct question. *Is omitting certain details for their own protection dishonest?* She looked away momentarily. "Let's keep the debate going. I'm open to reconsidering," said Joy. "You and I are the only ones with complete knowledge at this point. We can't let that knowledge die with us."

The profundity of the situation hit home for Joy. It was hard to fathom that once she and Robin were gone, an entire community of humans would never have known life outside of captivity. Despite being locked up now, she was grateful to have had a previous life. "What do you miss the most about your life, Robin?"

"Just about everything." Robin let out a deep sigh. "I took it all for granted. If I had to pick one thing though, it would have to be making plans and then implementing them: med school, work, travel. Even a simple plan, like spontaneously messaging a friend to meet for coffee and just heading out the door to join them. What do you miss the most, Joy?"

"Well, I had been watching the *Sunset Bay* series, and was nearing the final episode. I've always wondered how it ended."

"Seriously, that's what you miss the most? A soap opera!"

"No, but it's what I pretend I miss the most. I dream up my own versions of the final episode, just to keep myself from going insane in here. If we ever find freedom, maybe I can become a script writer instead of a Space Engineer."

"Not *if* we get out of here," said Robin, smiling reassuringly. *"When."*

CHAPTER 5

Adnil woke to the sound of heavy rain falling in the yard. The window was fogged up, condensation preventing a clear view into the yard. The damp air was musty and chilly, so she remained curled up in the bunk, pulling the two thin blankets tightly around her neck. When the bell sounded, she joined the lineup at the toilets—sometimes you just had to go!

When Adnil heard the door of the medical room open, she quickly got off the toilet and positioned herself at a station. Two commanders entering at the same time sometimes meant trouble. Adnil's shoulders tightened as the commanders walked up and down the rows of stations, scanning the area with their big yellow eyes and ensuring everything was in good order. Adnil felt their glare as they checked the breast pumps and the breasts. The commanders never looked a woman directly in the eye. In their presence, Adnil felt she was a body, without a mind or a soul.

With her head angled as she ate, Adnil was able to keep her head down and shift her eyes to the right and left to see the floor behind her. Her heart pounded as the long legs of a commander walked behind her, its large feet stepping in robotic rhythm. Her heart pounded faster when one of them paused directly behind her. Adnil held her breath, but to her relief, the long, alien legs moved along. The commanders eventually stopped behind Joy. Adnil noticed that Joy's station had not released any food today.

Is there something wrong with the hoses in that station? Adnil wondered hopefully. *Is that why the commanders are here? To repair a mechanical malfunction?* One of the commanders scanned its wristband across the digital reader, unlocking the clamp around Joy's wrist. It removed the pumps from Joy's breasts, then took Joy by the arm, guiding her towards the medical room. Joy turned, and her eyes met Adnil's. Adnil hoped Joy was just being removed for a routine medical exam and would be returned to the compound shortly, but somehow she knew she would likely never see Joy again.

CHAPTER 6

Joy's legs trembled as the commanders led her out, knowing that once she left the compound, she would never return. Her milk had run dry; her days of producing milk were over and she was of no use to them. She turned to look back at those she was leaving behind, and her eyes met Adnil's. Joy got along well with all the women in the compound and she had tried hard to create a sense of community despite the fact that they were living in bondage. However, she felt a special connection with Adnil. Adnil was quiet and unassuming, yet at the same time carried understated confidence. She absorbed information with a curious passion—a pleasure to have in the education sessions. Joy cherished the long conversations she and Adnil had had in the yard, sharing the same wonder and fascination of the sky and the glory it displayed. Joy felt a lump in her throat. She regretted not saying a proper goodbye to her friend.

A commander's hand tightly gripped Joy's wrist as the three of them reached the door. Her reluctant feet shuffled apprehensively as she was escorted into, and through, the medical room. They continued through a couple of connected rooms and then through a final exit door.

The shock of seeing the outside world froze Joy into a statue. Her heart raced as the vast space both amazed her and made her feel anxious. A flashback of her last time in the outside world came over her as she felt the same firm grip around her wrists today as when she was originally captured. She had just left her favourite campus pub where she had been socializing with schoolmates. Full of hopes and dreams for the future, they had been sharing post-graduate plans. The Xplerians came out of nowhere, captured her, and brought her to the compound. She had lived in this compound all the years since, and today she was leaving it.

The outside world looked foreign to her now. It was so colourful out here after the drabness of the dirt yard, where nothing grew except a few brave dandelions. The green of the leaves on a small tree and the two small bushes on either side of it were brighter than the green she had in her memory.

Joy felt a stick prodding her in the back as one of the commanders tried to coax her to start walking again. Frozen with fear, her feet did not move. In frustration, the commanders yanked her arms, pulling her forward. The action snapped her back to the present, and she reluctantly took a few steps. Focussing ahead, she saw they were leading her towards a windowless white cargo van, similar to the one she was thrown into years ago. In a panic, she managed to free her wrist and run. A commander caught her almost immediately, thanks to its long alien legs. Joy shrieked as the commander grabbed her hair, then collapsed to the ground in defeat. Despair washed over her while hope for a bright future vanished like a solar eclipse.

The commander dragged her to her feet, holding her more firmly, arms awkwardly forced behind her back. She felt the tight grip of long fingers securely wrapped around both wrists. Her arms burned and the top of her scalp stung as one of the commanders locked on to a fist full of hair for a secure grip. Her body jolted as the point of the stick jabbed deeply into her back.

With no further delays, the commanders manoeuvred her to the vehicle. The back doors opened, and she was shoved inside. Lying on the hard floor in darkness, she felt the vibration of the vehicle as it buzzed down the road. Unlike her original journey in a white van, she was its only passenger. Living in the compound's tight quarters, she hadn't been alone in eons. The desolation of the spacious cargo van was immense, like a bottomless pit. After a long journey to the unknown, the vehicle stopped. The back door opened, and the commanders motioned she should exit. Wanting to avoid being dragged out, she cooperated. The bright light offended her eyes as she took in her surroundings. As her eyes adjusted, she could make out numerous buildings. The pit in her stomach hardened as the commanders led her towards the door of one of them. *What will happen to me in there? Will I be killed?*

Using its wristband, a commander released the lock and led Joy through a series of small rooms. Once through the final door, Joy heard the familiar *click* of the door closing and locking behind her.

Joy stood still, her eyes scanning her new environs. Morning light penetrated the otherwise dark compound through a couple of windows facing an adjoining yard. It was similar in some ways to the compound she had just left. Joy could see that it had an area full of stacked bunks that opened to the main area containing rows of long tables and stools. There were food dispensers at each station, but none of the hoses and other paraphernalia used for milking.

The place was dotted with girls of varying heights, dressed in yellow tunics. Some lay sleeping in bunks while others sat on stools, waiting for food to be dispensed. A few children sat on the floor interacting with a stick, seemingly unaware of the new arrival. Some stood against a wall, eyes glazed, looking straight ahead, while others sat on the floor, rocking silently, ignoring those who were busy arguing with the air. A couple of the smallest children noticed Joy's presence, looking at her with mild curiosity.

Joy eventually made her way to a stool and sat down. Tears welled up in her eyes, waiting for the floodgates to open and release the backlog of emotional pain. Once again, she had been plucked from her community. The agony of being torn away from her friends and brought here against her will stung her soul. The sight of the pitiful, innocent girls—who had no idea that their lives were only going to get worse—broke her heart. Trying to maintain her composure for the sake of the children, she buried her face in her hands to hide the despair it would show and closed her eyes. She didn't want the children's first encounter with her to include witnessing a strange, hysterical adult unravelling cathartically before them. Mourning the loss of dear friends would have to be delayed.

A bell sounded, prompting the children to run to the feed stations. Joy sat quietly and watched as food was dispensed into a basin in front of each stool. The girls were not tied down and could eat freely with both hands. The children looked physically healthy; they had a good weight, their skin was clear and free from sores, and although matted, they had full heads of hair. But their vacant eyes lacked sparkle.

Joy was unsure whether she was housed here temporarily or if it was permanent. In the meantime, she found a vacant bunk to sleep in and joined the children for food every time the bell rang. The rest of the time was spent observing and waiting.

Joy watched as a toddler struggled with her tunic. Somehow she had managed to get the clothing partially removed, but it was twisted and stuck over her face, causing great frustration and loud, angry screaming. The eyes of several girls turned towards Joy with a look of expectation, like they assumed she would tame the tumultuous child. It was becoming evident that her new role was to take care of the children. *Am I a replacement for their previous caregiver?* The children seemed to know the answer to this already, expectation in their orphan eyes.

With mixed feelings, Joy submitted to the new role: to care for the girls in this compound until they were mature and ready to be moved on. After producing their first offspring, each child would be relocated to an adult compound, where they would spend the rest of their life as milkers.

Joy pondered where to start with this monumental task as she quietly observed the children after an evening feeding session. *How can I make a difference in their bleak lives? Can I create a fictitious, kind world inside the broader, cruel world? Would that be misleading?*

Joy knew her protective bubble had a unique expiration date for each child, and eventually they would be subjected to their destiny. But what other option did she have? All she could do was hope they would be released before too many of them experienced the dreadful life of a milker.

Joy painted on a cheerful smile, drew in a deep breath, and started to sing. Her voice exuded gentleness, like soft clouds on a warm spring day. A bright, joyous melody radiated up from her soul and out through her mouth. It was the first of many songs she would sing for the children.

CHAPTER 7

Adnil mindlessly placed one foot in front of the other, trudging in endless circles. She had been moping for days since Joy was abruptly removed from the compound. Her insides ached and felt hollow, like she had part of her soul cut out. Not even the appearance of the orange cat silhouetted against a bright blue sky could interest her. Joy had brought a ray of happiness into Adnil's bleak, morose existence. Joy had beamed hope like a rainbow emerging after a rainstorm. But in an instant, she had been scooped away.

A milker could be taken to the medical room for a variety of reasons, including a vaginal probe, treatment for mastitis or another infection, or to have the baby extracted from her growing belly, but she always returned to the compound. However, a milker past her prime, who permanently dried up, was no longer useful to the commanders, and the originals were fading fast. There was only one left. After an evening milking session, Adnil stood in the spot between the rows of stations where Joy had always positioned herself when speaking. The group had not resumed the education sessions since Joy's removal. Everyone was too melancholic and needed a break from the sessions.

Adnil missed her friend. She missed her nurturing manner as she spoke at the sessions. She missed her positive attitude and hope for the future. She missed her gentleness and the private moments they often shared in the yard. Adnil thought more about the discussion when Joy had urged Adnil to consider becoming a teacher. *Without real-life experience in the outside world, do I have enough of a knowledge base? Would the women listen to me?* Adnil did not know if she would be able to give the women hope for a better future the way Joy had. She was not even sure Joy's hope for the future was realistic.

The door to the compound suddenly opened and Adnil watched as a petite human was pushed through. The newcomer's wavy orange hair framed her pale face, which was many shades lighter than Adnil's tan skin. Freckles were scattered across her face like stars in the night sky. Her eyes, the colour of the sky on a clear day, were intense with fear as she entered the compound. The new arrival was barely past childhood herself, yet old enough to have given birth to a baby, making her a primip, able to produce milk and ready to join the adult compound—finally useful to the Xplerians.

The new arrival was dressed in the standard uniform: green tunic, green socks, and brown shoes. Her left wrist displayed the requisite wristband. Like all new arrivals, she came with no name, only a number. Her thin arms held two blankets and an extra pair of socks.

The women welcomed the new arrivals as best they could, trying to make them feel welcome and safe. However, not everyone was happy when newcomers arrived. The shortage of bunks often meant that someone would have to give up her bunk and sleep on the floor.

Observing this new arrival, Adnil remembered Joy's words of compassion: "Life is harsh enough for them without us making it worse. New arrivals have just experienced the trauma of undergoing their first extraction. We must treat them with kindness."

Adnil usually left the welcoming of new arrivals to others, but Joy's guiding words resonated with her this time and she was quick to take on the welcoming role. Language skills of newcomers were usually rudimentary—Adnil didn't remember speaking much herself as a child—there was very little interaction and certainly no education sessions. Adnil gave the brief orientation using hand gestures and a demonstrating manner.

Adnil felt compassion for the new arrival. She remembered the terror she felt the day of her own first extraction, and how she was shoved through a door into this place after the ordeal instead of going back to her regular quarters. She pitied the way the new arrival was abandoned at the door, with no awareness of the next phase of her life or the expectations that came with it.

Sometimes new arrivals stayed in bed for several days, crying quietly and not wanting to associate with the others. But eventually they surrendered to their destiny and participated in milkings, because it was the only way to obtain food in this compound.

#

The floor felt hard against Adnil's hip bone, but the softness she felt in her heart for giving up her bunk to the new arrival almost made up for it. Almost. *I wish I had more than two measly blankets.* She closed her eyes and envisioned an enormous pile of blankets stacked so high she wouldn't even be able to feel a pebble under them. She thought more about Joy's assurance that they would one day be released. If it were to happen, she would never again have to sleep on a cold, hard floor.

In the morning, the new arrival followed Adnil to the milking area and sat at the station beside her. She watched as Adnil opened the front of her tunic and attached the funnel cups to her breasts, mimicking each step and ultimately bringing the dispensed food to her mouth with her right hand. Hungry, she quickly ate it all. Adnil looked over at her and smiled reassuringly. The new arrival with the bright blue eyes smiled back with gratitude. The newcomer spent a lot of time with Adnil over the next few days, following her around the compound and mimicking her actions. One bright, clear day, the two were sharing a moment in the yard, looking up at the sky, trying to pick out the most uniquely shaped clouds. "Oh look, that ugly one looks like a commander's head," said Adnil, and they both laughed.

The sky was brilliant blue, the same colour as the new arrival's eyes.

"That's what your name will be!" exclaimed Adnil, moved by the inspiration. "*Sky* is the perfect name for you." Adnil reached out her hand and gently touched Sky's cheek.

Sky smiled. "Thank you. I like the name you gave me."

CHAPTER 8

As a commander entered the compound during a morning milking session, Adnil kept her head low, inches from the food in front of her, trying to remain less noticeable. As it paced behind her, she watched the floor without moving her head. Her heart sank when she saw the long legs stop directly behind her. The rest of the milking session seemed to take forever as it waited for her to finish, yet at the same time it wasn't long enough. Her hand trembled slightly as it brought the remaining food to her mouth. When the milk ceased flowing, the clamp holding Adnil's wrist in place released, and the commander motioned for her to stand up. Taking her by the forearm, it led her to the medical room.

Adnil was always shocked at how different this room was from where she spent most of her time. Unlike the rest of the compound, the medical room was very clean and shiny, with bright lights reflecting off the stainless steel and casting harsh artificial illumination. The air smelled clean and sterile, but not in a wholesome way.

The commander motioned for Adnil to disrobe. She obeyed, placing the tunic on a stool; it appeared filthy in contrast to the cleanliness of the stool. The commander motioned for Adnil to sit on the examination table. Hooking a finger under her jaw, it forced her chin upward for a better view. Adnil felt her bottom lip pinched between long, boney fingers as it tugged her lip down for a closer inspection. The assault from the alien fingers continued as it pulled down an eyelid, pressed hard on her belly, and squeezed her breasts. Without emotion, the commander pointed for Adnil to lie on her back. Knowing what was coming next, she spread her legs apart and closed her eyes. She had learned, the hard way, that not cooperating turned a bad experience into a terrible experience.

Behind closed eyelids, Adnil disappeared into her mind, seeking refuge in another world. She envisioned herself running like the wind in a world without walls. Joy had said that Adnil was fortunate to have her mind's eye to paint a picture of captivating sanctuaries, that a small minority of people with a neurological condition called aphantasia were not able to conjure mental images, instead encoding information as data. Adnil did not know how she would have coped all this time without the liberating sanctuaries she pictured with her third eye.

"Wouldn't a person who can't picture imaginary worlds really miss it?" she had asked Joy.

"You can't miss something if you don't know it exists," Joy had responded. "And you function just as well without it. I don't remember people in the outside world talking about it much. Those who experience mental imagery take it for granted because they assume everyone has the ability."

Adnil frequently found respite within her mind. Her favourite scene was running through meadows and other interesting places she had learned about in education sessions. Today, as the commander's work continued between her legs, she imagined herself as a long-distance runner in a world competition. Being a fast runner with remarkable endurance, she held a considerable lead in the race. She felt her whole body working: her leg muscles were warm, fresh air entered her lungs, and blood flowed into all her limbs. Glancing over her right shoulder, she could see a competitor gaining on her. Moments later, she could hear their breath. Adrenaline coursed through her veins. Digging deep, she found some reserve energy to increase the gap between them.

A yank on her arm jolted Adnil out of the escape-dream and into miserable reality. With the task finished, the commander directed Adnil to stand in the corner above a drain hole in the floor. Adnil recoiled when the frigid water hit her body, then stood rigid while the commander hosed her down. Despite the initial shock, she welcomed having her entire body washed. The only water supply in the compound was the drinking fountain, which they occasionally used to wash their face and hands, especially on warm summer days.

The spraying stopped, and a dry towel was thrown at her. The fabric felt fabulously foreign against her skin as it absorbed the water. Before she was finished patting herself dry, the towel was pulled away. White powder showered down on her as the commander gave her a good delousing. Adnil coughed as the fine particles stung her throat and lungs, leaving a bitter taste in her mouth. The dirty tunic stuck to her in spots where her body was still wet as she struggled to put it back on. Scanning its wristband, the commander unlocked the door and pushed Adnil back into the compound. Still cold and slightly damp, Adnil walked to the bunk area. Sky was lying in the bunk, so Adnil took one of the blankets and spread it out on the floor.

"There you are," said Sky. Her kind eyes met Adnil's, and she gestured for Adnil to join her on the bunk.

It was a tight squeeze with both of them in the bunk, but Adnil preferred it to lying on the hard floor. With the front of her body pressed against Sky's back, Adnil wrapped her arms around Sky's small, delicate frame, appreciating the warmth emanating from her body. She buried her face in the back of Sky's head, biting her lower lip in an effort to hold back the tears that were knocking at her eyelids' doors. They lay motionless in sad silence for some time until Sky rolled over to face Adnil.

Adnil felt Sky's gaze linger—the type of empathetic eyes that go right into your soul. Bringing her face closer to Adnil's, Sky instinctively pressed her mouth against Adnil's passive lips. It felt soft, comforting, and inviting to Adnil. Sky pressed her mouth against Adnil's lips a second time, and Adnil welcomed the intimate gesture with intrigue. The novel sensation triggered a spark, an unfamiliar raw feeling of delightful yearning that had been lying dormant. Adnil reciprocated with a tender kiss, which was received by Sky with parted lips, eliciting a strange and heightened arousal within Adnil.

The tactile exploration continued, migrating to other body parts, igniting the latent desire further. The amorous passion deepened as they touched each other's bodies, multiplying with each new territory explored, until they reached a pleasurable zone they never knew existed. They fell asleep in each other's arms, eventually waking from the slumber in slow motion as they transitioned from their peaceful, euphoric sleep back to reality.

Sky smiled. "We will have to share the bunk more often, especially on cool nights. After all, four blankets are better than two."

"Yes, for sure," replied Adnil. The pooling of resources was less important than the intimate odyssey they had shared. Before this moment, she had thought her body belonged to the commanders—an object used for their gain. Now she knew it was much more than that.

From then on, the two shared a bunk every night.

CHAPTER 9

A blanket of fresh white snow brought a sense of joy and frivolity to the compound yard, distracting the milkers from their reality by showcasing the miracle of nature in all its wonder. Although their milker shoes were inadequate for the rare weather event, Adnil and Sky tramped through the snowy yard. Any feelings of bitterness about their lot in life were momentarily transformed into feelings of curiosity and adventure.

"Duck down, Adnil!" Sky's warning was too late, as a soft snowball hit the back of her head, exploding into smithereens on impact.

Retaliation time. Adnil eagerly reached down to form a snowball and fired it back at the instigator.

Robin couldn't help laughing, thinking of her childhood school days. But the bell signalling milking time broke up the fun and summoned everyone inside.

Other than rising for the midnight milking and feeding, Adnil slept soundly through the night, pressed tightly against Sky's warm body. They woke before the morning bell and rushed to the window to see if the snow had stuck around. Adnil scratched the frost off the window to create a peep hole.

"The snow is even higher today!" exclaimed Sky.

It continued dumping snow for days. The falling snowflakes made Adnil pause and take notice of each flake as it gently landed in the yard. They piled up on top of one another to create a growing blanket of snow. Her recent feelings of nausea melted away as she took in the beauty of the snow and breathed in the crisp air. Adnil knew from education sessions that snow meant the air was colder, but somehow it felt less cold outside now compared to the usual drizzly days. Maybe it was the novelty of the snow, or maybe it was the energy exerted when firing snowballs at Valda's head, but somehow Adnil felt warmer.

"If the snow gets any higher, we might be able to step over the wall," joked Aaron.

The snow disappeared as fast as it arrived, melting into a field of slushy mud during a sudden warm spell. The joyful mood thawed to disappointment as they lamented the loss of the clean snow and refrained from entering the muddy yard.

Then the rain came. It poured for days, unceasingly. The ground was unable to soak it up, causing pools of muddy water to form. Adnil watched the raindrops as they landed, each drop losing its individuality as it became part of the opaque collective.

"I've witnessed phenomena like this," said Robin with a worried look, then muttered under her breath: "Atmospheric river, pineapple express, aqua dome, super torrent."

The water rose higher and higher until it no longer remained in the yard, but ventured into the compound.

"Flood waters can harbour bacteria and disease-carrying organisms," warned Robin. "Keep your hands clean and don't touch your mouth or eyes."

Adnil sloshed through the ankle-deep water to and from the milking stations, but otherwise remained in the bunk, high and dry. Her boring days became even more mind-numbing without education sessions or time spent in the yard. Sky's fidgeting and scratching of a scab irritated her; the constant physical closeness was starting to lose its appeal.

"Thank goodness we are safe on the top bunk," said Sky with a scratchy voice.

Sky's fidgeting was soon accompanied by chills. Adnil touched Sky's hot forehead and felt a twinge of guilt for feeling bothered by the fidgeting.

Adnil looked up at the ceiling and felt it closing in on her. Normally this sensation would prompt her to go to the yard for some fresh air, but not today. Adnil closed her eyes and concentrated hard so she wouldn't vomit. She didn't feel like wading through the water to get to the toilet right now. But the demon had its own unconstrained agenda. Down the bunk she climbed, into water that was now just below her knees. Adnil reached the toilet just in time, and the bitter puke erupted with determination—leaving her with a relieved stomach but a vile taste in her mouth. She took a sip from the water fountain and swished it around her mouth in an attempt to cleanse the lingering memento.

"How long do you think this will last?" she asked Robin on the way back to her bunk. Adnil kept her voice to a whisper as she gestured vaguely. "I can't take it much longer, and Sky is sick."

"You'll know when the turning point is here. At some point, the water level will plateau, then change direction."

"Where are the commanders? Aren't they going to come and save us?" asked Sky upon Adnil's return.

Adnil felt torn. She too hoped the commanders would realize their commodity was in danger and take steps to remove them from harm's way. But she wasn't sure she wanted them to discover Sky unwell, knowing their tolerance for sick humans was low. Robin had said the business of keeping perishable commodities was a risky operation. Decisions required constant cost-benefit analysis. Maintaining a sick milker came at a cost, and the treatment had to be seen as worth the extra investment.

The knot tightened in Adnil's stomach. Between the worry and the nausea, she wasn't eating or sleeping much. And her overactive mind played out all the possible scenarios, driving her deeper and deeper into a state of helplessness. *The commanders will rescue us from the rising waters; they will notice Sky is sick and take her to the medical room for treatment. But what if she's removed permanently?* This slim possibility concerned Adnil. Her soul would die if she lost Sky. *Obviously she is much too valuable to discard. She is young with many milking days ahead of her.*

Exhausted, Adnil's mind finally succumbed to a long solid sleep. She was jolted awake by the sound of the bell. Her reluctant eyes remained closed as she wondered what time of day it was, and which of the four milkings she was being summoned to. Her eyes opened cautiously, peering through little slits, gradually focussing on the ceiling above. The musty smell of the flood waters brought her back to reality. She turned and gazed at Sky, who was awake and humming softly. Her chills had subsided. Hungry, Adnil climbed down the bunk and stepped onto the flooded floor, relieved to find the water had receded and was now only ankle-deep. Morning light shone through the dirty window, lifting her spirits. *Finally, things are going in the right direction.*

CHAPTER 10

The group that stayed for the education session appeared noticeably larger than it had when Robin first restarted them. *Looks like they are beginning to accept me*, she thought with relief. Robin knew they missed Joy dearly, and she could never replace her; however, as the last original, she was the only one fully equipped to lead the education sessions. She knew she should mentor one of the others, but couldn't yet face what that would actually mean.

Robin remembered the dreadful day, three weeks before she was to start her second year of medical school. She was heading home from her part-time job at the Garden Centre when she was captured and thrown into the back of a white vehicle. Years of education down the drain. But now, many years later, in this surreal situation, she was able to share some of her knowledge. Like Joy, Robin never lost hope for being released and saw the value in educating the women—despite not knowing whether the education would ever serve a practical purpose.

While Joy's lectures took a general tone, with sensitive topics omitted, Robin chose not to hold back on details, even if the truth hurt. Until recently, the women had been unschooled about males and the role they played in human reproduction. Nobody in the compound had connected the dots about what actually caused lactation, either. Such ignorance of how your own body functioned would have been shocking to Robin before colonization, but being born in captivity and living your life in a locked enclosure changed everything. Today, Robin would connect the dots.

"In some species, the male is larger and physically stronger than the female," explained Robin, "but most species, including humans, have evolved to be monomorphic, resulting in males and females being of equal size and having equal strength. Although there are more similarities than differences, each sex has unique body parts that must physically connect in order to produce an offspring."

Robin discussed the anatomy specific to each sex: vagina, penis, womb, breasts. "Although rare, humans can be born with both male and female anatomy."

"So you mean one person can be a combination of male and female?" asked Adnil with piqued curiosity.

"Yes."

"So the commanders are male, right?" asked Aaron.

"Not necessarily. Why would you assume that?" said Robin.

"Well, you said females are the ones with breasts. I haven't seen a commander with breasts, so they must be male," said Aaron.

Robin smiled at the simple conclusion as she recalled learning about similar misconceptions in an *Ancient Medical Myths* course in university. "The commanders are a different species, so we can't compare their body parts to human ones," she explained. "Also, because we are forced into a continual cycle of pregnancy and lactation, and likely fed a concoction of hormones, our breasts are artificially enlarged. If we were wild women in the natural world, they would be smaller."

Robin elaborated on reproduction in the natural world, explaining exactly how the penis and vagina united to create a miniature human that formed inside the host until it was ready to enter the world.

"What the freak are you saying?" A wide-eyed recent arrival, face flushing, seemed to be having trouble processing the new information.

All the women were aware that they became pregnant via the vaginal injection in the medical room; but other than the originals, nobody was aware that the magic seed inserted by the commanders was stolen from their own kind.

Robin realized the whole truth would be hard to accept for some. *Males* were foreign to them, and they hardly knew what a *baby* was—even though they were popping them out every couple of years, like acorns falling from a tree in a heavy wind. The disconnect between them and the creature tethered to them during its formation was obvious. They never really saw the newborn. If they were curious, they might be able to catch a glimpse of the creature as it was extracted and taken to the other side of the curtain. But most women were disinterested and, assisted by drugs, detached from the whole process. They just wanted to get the process over with so they could return to the compound. They had been aware they were a commodity, trapped in a manufactured environment so Xplerians could steal their milk, but this new layer of information about male humans made the whole thing appear even more sick and twisted.

Adnil's brain churned. *How come I never heard of males before? Why didn't Joy mention their existence*? Out loud she asked, "Where are the males kept?"

"That is a mystery to us," replied Robin. "Aside from harvesting their sperm, we are not sure if there is another purpose for them or even how many there are."

"While we're trapped in this hole, we will never know," said Valda.

"Maybe we'll find out sooner than ya think," said Dawn, sending Valda an impatient look.

During subsequent sessions, Robin expanded on how the women were on a continuous cycle of pregnancies in order to keep the milk flowing. "Our mammary glands produce milk meant to feed our babies, but the milk is taken from us just like our newborns are stolen from us."

"So, milk … is supposed to be food for newborn humans?" asked Aaron, in surprise. "Holy Freak! What are the yellow-eyed monsters wanting it for?"

"We don't know," admitted Robin.

There had been much debate among the teachers about how much information should be divulged. Joy didn't see how it would benefit the milkers. But Robin thought it was important for the women to know the full truth. It was convenient for Xplerians if milkers remained ignorant, cooperative, and didn't question things, but she would not give in to that. With the privilege of being a knowledge keeper came responsibility and Robin thought she should share everything in her knowledge bank, especially now that she was the last remaining original in the compound.

#

Adnil was not sure how she felt about this new information. It certainly didn't make her feel any better, and she didn't see how it would change her situation. She felt the fetus inside her move. It did not belong to her. She was owned by the commanders—as was the creature in her belly and the milk in her breasts.

CHAPTER 11

Adnil woke to a chorus of birds welcoming the arrival of the morning light. The musical chatter began as a boisterous cacophony, but as choir members began dropping out one by one, Adnil could pick out individual songbird notes. With Sky already out of bed, Adnil repositioned herself onto her side, luxuriously taking up the entire width of the bunk, with ample room for her growing belly. She closed her eyes, blocking out the drab surroundings. The sound of the remaining birds trilling added a ray of joy and peace to her inner sanctum. Adnil identified the song of a robin, clearly a sign that the cold season was behind them. The bird's jubilant warble lifted her heart and refreshed her spirit. As the choir dwindled and the final soloist bowed out, Adnil abandoned her bunk and went to find Sky.

The cool days had dragged on endlessly, with many full moons coming and going during the cold season. Finally, a reprieve, bringing lingering light and the promise of warmer days.

Sky was in the yard, bent over and cradling something in her hands. As Adnil got closer, she could see a small mouse lying motionless in Sky's hands.

"It's not moving. What's wrong with it?" Sky's voice resonated with worry. The animal was clearly dead, but Adnil did not answer right away. In the compound, there was little opportunity for direct experience with death. Since women were removed from the compound when their milk dried up, milkers never witnessed others growing very old, let alone dying. The only dead creatures they encountered were occasional dried-up insects, like the spiders they sometimes found on the floor, curled up into lifeless little balls.

Adnil remembered Robin's words about honesty: a truthful response to a direct question is always fair. "It's dead," she finally responded. "Just like that spider we saw the other day that wasn't moving."

"So it will never wake up again, right?"

"I think that's right."

"Will we be dead one day too?" Sky asked as she looked up at Adnil with concern.

"Yes, we will, but I don't know much about death," answered Adnil truthfully. She put her hand on Sky's shoulder. "We'll have to ask Robin to tell us more about it."

It started to rain. Sky covered the furry, limp mouse with her second hand to prevent it from getting wet. "I don't want to be here."

"Do you want to go inside?"

"No, I mean, I no longer want to live in this compound."

Adnil, unable to come up with a response adequate enough to relieve Sky's distress, said nothing.

"Sometimes at night," continued Sky, "I dream that we are wild, living without walls, in a place where milking sessions don't exist. Dawn said it will happen one day."

Adnil's heart sank, wishing desperately there was something she could do to give Sky a better future. She worried that Dawn had given Sky false hope. She stood in silence, watching Sky with her delicate hands cupped around the dead mouse, until the bell rang for the morning milking session. Sky laid the dead mouse in a corner of the yard, and the two of them covered it with some stones.

"We better go in now; we can come back later and give it a proper burial," said Adnil.

Sky glanced at Adnil dubiously. However, there was no time to linger and discuss this unfamiliar procedure further, so they made their way inside. Most of the others were already assembled at the stations and had started milking. Adnil and Sky found two empty spots about ten stations apart and began the milking routine. Adnil was hungry and quickly started eating the dispensed food.

Shortly after they were settled at their stations, Adnil heard the metal door open. As usual, she kept her head down as the commander clomped behind the women. When the footsteps stopped, Adnil looked up to see who today's victim was. It was Sky. Adnil sat, powerless, still attached to the funnel cups, as she watched Sky being guided towards the medical room. She wanted to run after them in an effort to protect Sky, but, even if her wrist wasn't still in the clamp, she knew such an action would be in vain, or could even make things worse for Sky.

Feeling despondent, Adnil skipped the education session and went to lie in the bunk. She kept glancing towards the door, anxious for Sky's return. But that made her even more anxious, so she retreated to the yard, pacing back and forth aimlessly—feeling helpless. There were a lot of things she hated about being confined to the compound, but the worst was the lack of control: a slave at the mercy of her master.

Sky returned and found Adnil near the pile of small stones, and the two of them sat silently beside the little mouse beneath it.

The burial can wait, thought Adnil, not wanting to put Sky through any more trauma.

Finally, Sky broke the silence.

"I think today's commander was a female."

"What makes you say that?"

"It's hard to know for certain, but I think those small mounds under the commander's uniform were breasts."

#

Sky and Adnil shared this speculation with others after the midday milking session. It led to a lively debate.

"One would think that if the commander is female, it would be able to relate to our plight," said Aaron.

"What damn difference does that make?" rebuked Valda. "Should a female commander be expected to feel guilty for keeping us as slaves, but we don't expect the same from the male commanders?"

"But Valda, the only reason we are locked up in this stinking compound is because we are female!" replied Aaron. "You'd think a female commander … with breasts … regardless of the species, would not stand for it. I feel betrayed."

"Oh come on! I don't buy that line of reasoning," countered Valda. "All the yellow-eyed monsters are equally guilty. It's not fair to expect empathy from a female commander but consider it okay that the male commanders are unapologetic for their actions."

"Are you defending the female commander?" questioned Aaron.

"I'm not defending anyone. I'm just saying that your argument suggests a female commander is somehow more guilty because it should know better, and that is shitty reasoning."

The heated debate continued throughout the day. It was not common for the women to argue. Occasionally there were minor conflicts over things such as someone taking too much time at the water fountain or at the toilet. And living in close quarters sometimes caused irritability, but for the most part, the women were mild-mannered and tolerant of one another. With their new insights from Robin, this was different; it brought out strong opinions.

In the late afternoon, Adnil and Sky returned to the yard to tend to the mouse, relieved to find it undisturbed. They found a spot away from the footpath suitable for a burial. The rain had made the ground soft enough for digging. Adnil's fingers scooped out soil until an ample burial hole was formed. Sky carefully lowered the lifeless creature down into the bed. Adnil covered it with dirt, pointing out to Sky that this would help to keep it undisturbed, then plucked a yellow dandelion that had recently emerged from its dormant nap and placed it on top of the grave. Like the fragile creature lying beneath the ground, the flower was a symbol of the fragility of life: coping with stress and adversity, striving to be resilient, yet at the mercy of proper conditions in order to reach its full potential.

Adnil placed her hand in Sky's as they stood in silence at the gravesite. The warmth of the sun on her face as it appeared from behind a cloud brought lightness to the melancholy moment.

"What will happen to the mouse now?" asked Sky.

"It will gradually decompose."

"Oh, now I remember. It's just like Robin told us in an education session. The body will break down and become part of the earth again."

"Yes, that's right." Adnil was relieved she did not have to explain it further. Having lived in the compound longer than Sky, she had heard many more of the recycled education sessions. She couldn't keep track of what topics Sky had knowledge about. Obviously burials were not one of them, but body decomposition was.

The shared experience of burying the dead mouse gave Adnil some satisfaction, a sense of closure, an honourable action they had done together. Opportunities like this were rare. Usually they waited for things to happen to them. This time they were the ones taking action towards another creature, only they chose to do it with dignity and respect.

Later that evening, while gazing up into the night sky, Adnil reflected more about the arguments that had occurred earlier. It was a particularly clear night with little cloud cover and low wind, which made for perfect sky-gazing conditions.

Robin wandered over to join Adnil. "Gee, it's peaceful out here. I had to get out. There's an excessive amount of chatter in there tonight."

"What an unusual day," said Adnil.

"Yes, it was."

"It is unfortunate that the women had such a heated argument over the female commander … We seldom have arguments," said Adnil.

"Well, it's not such a bad thing," said Robin. "The fact that we can disagree and have a healthy debate is a sign of independent thinking and active minds. Frankly, I found it refreshing."

"I never thought of it that way," said Adnil.

"In our regimented life with virtually no decisions to make, there isn't much opportunity to express one's point of view on anything," said Robin. "It's nice to see that we can have strong opinions about topics."

"Well that's a good way of looking at it. There certainly were strong opinions and healthy minds debating today."

"For sure! We're not the docile, mindless milkers that the Xplerians think we are," Robin concluded enthusiastically.

The following morning, towards the end of the milking session, the commander of interest entered the compound. The commander paused for a moment as all eyes turned towards it. Fidgeting uncomfortably, it pulled the collar of the blue uniform upward as if subconsciously trying to escape into it. There was no lingering today. Instead of taking time to pace around and do a general inspection, it went directly to today's target: Valda.

A rumble of murmurs and whispers spread across the compound like faint thunder from a faraway storm. All eyes were on Valda as the commander led her away. Halfway across the room, Valda turned and looked back with a satisfied smirk on her face, as if she had been carefully selected to go on an important mission to discover the truth. Dawn let out a giggle, which swept through the whole compound like a gust of wind until everyone was laughing uncontrollably. The bemused commander nervously swiped the reader and led Valda through the door to the medical room, quickly closing it behind them.

The women waited eagerly for Valda's return, curious to hear the report. Valda's time in the medical room was much shorter than most visits.

"Well, what did you find out?" asked Dawn.

"Yes, she definitely has breasts. Apart from that, she appears no different from the other commander. But I definitely think she is a female—at this moment anyway."

"What do you mean, at this moment?" said Aaron.

"Well, maybe it is something that changes, you know, depending on what you get exposed to," said Valda.

"I never heard of that," said Adnil.

"So, anything you haven't heard of can't be true?" said Valda. "In case you haven't noticed, we are locked up in a compound and are very limited in things we hear about."

"You're right, Valda. Some species do not adhere to a gender binary," said Robin.

"What the heck does that mean, Robin?" said Aaron with heightened curiosity.

"It means they don't stick to being female or male their whole life, they can switch sexes," said Robin. "For example, clownfish all begin life as male, but they carry both female and male reproductive organs. The leader is a female. When the dominant female dies, her mate takes her place and changes its sex to female."

"Wouldn't it be great to be able to choose!" said Adnil.

"What do clownfish have to do with the Xplerians?" said Aaron.

"Well, if it is possible for clownfish to change their sex, it could very well be possible for other species such as Xplerians. We can't rule it out," said Robin.

"Enough about that. There are more important things that I discovered today," said Valda. "I took something from the medical room." She reached into her matted hair and pulled out a small medical tool. "I will add it to my collection. This weapon might come in handy one day," she uttered, sounding like a prisoner making plans for an escape as she proudly marched out to the yard.

CHAPTER 12

Due to her large belly, it was getting crowded with two in the bunk, and between that and the heat, Adnil was hardly sleeping. It was nearly time for another visit to the medical room for an extraction—her third. Despite being apprehensive about the procedure, she was eager to rid her body of the invasive burden.

Adnil felt a trickle of sweat roll down her forehead as she lay in the bunk alone one afternoon. The air was thick and hot. The sound of flies buzzing around her face was irritating but not wanting to generate more heat through movement, she did not swat them away. The only other movement was the restless lifeform inside her. Perhaps it too had had enough of its environment and wanted relief. *Augh*! *Let's just get this removal over with*, thought Adnil as she tried to ignore a fly that landed on her face.

#

The cool air in the medical room made it feel like Adnil had been transported to another season. She concentrated on the cold, hard examination table against her aching back as the commander picked up her arm with the wristband and scanned it across the reader beside her. A clamp opened up around Adnil's wrist, then clicked, locking her in place.

After arranging some tools on a small table, the commander's long alien fingers gestured for Adnil to place her feet in the stirrups, where they too were locked in place. She swallowed the red pill placed in her mouth and began to relax. Her head felt foggy, but not so much that she was unaware of what was going on around her. Unlike previous visits, where she would close her eyes and escape into her mind, this time she tried to stay alert and aware of the surroundings. Valda had been talking about the importance of gathering information about the medical room—something about it being critical to formulating their exit plan. Adnil wasn't sure whether to take Valda seriously. Adnil doubted an escape would ever happen, and thought there was a greater chance that they would one day be released, just like Joy had always said.

However, just in case, Adnil thought she might as well do what she could to contribute. Fighting off the drowsiness, she looked around the windowless room, trying to carve a picture in her mind so she could share the details with Valda later. A white curtain blocked her view of the far end of the room. Besides the door leading back to the compound, Adnil made note of a second door, wondering if that one led to the outside world. Two similar doors, yet what was on the other side was so different: one leading to a lifetime of misery, the other to wide open space and possibilities.

Adnil swallowed the second pill she was given. This one was green and softer than the first. The commander operated a hand-held machine that made beeping sounds as it was moved over Adnil's body. Near it was a square with brightly lit letters and numbers walking across it. Adnil felt the creature move lower in her body in preparation to exit.

Despite the lure of drowsiness, Adnil continued to scan the room for useful information. Through sleepy eyes, she saw rows of bottles lining shelves on the wall. She also saw a variety of medical tools. Some of them might have been similar to the one Valda had stolen, but she couldn't be sure. She wondered if the effort of lifting items from the medical room was worth the risk of getting caught.

Adnil tried to block out the presence of the blue uniform standing between the stirrups as the wide end of a hose was pressed up against her for the extraction. It felt like the creature was now even lower in her body, part way down the canal and on its way out of her body. She would soon be rid of it. With a press of a button on the machine, the suction hose began pulling its target. Although in a light fog, Adnil was mindful of the thing being withdrawn from her. She looked down the length of her body, trying to get a good look as it exited her body. It was the first time she had actually watched an extraction. The chubby-cheeked creature had dark hair just like hers. Its skin looked mottled and wet. Adnil saw little arms moving about.

The commander wrapped its long alien fingers around its ankles and carried it to the area with the drain in the floor. Holding it upside down using one hand, the commander operated the water hose with the other hand. The tiny creature let out an ear-piercing wail oddly disproportionate to its size. Adnil recalled being hosed off, the sudden pressure of the cold water against her body and how she had recoiled in shock at the abruptness of it. *How can the tiny creature withstand the pressure?* Adnil shuddered, unexpectedly feeling overwhelming concern for the infant.

The commander paid no attention to the shrieking and continued with the task. Adnil witnessed the infant's skin turn red with the exception of its bluish hands and feet. Once finished, the creature was wrapped in a green blanket. Adnil could see the exposed face: reddish, except for a distinct brown birthmark on its forehead, shaped like a crescent moon.

Like a lunar eclipse, the creature disappeared out of sight, and Adnil's eyes welled with tears. The piercing cry on the other side of the curtain rattled her eardrums, and she marvelled at how a tiny creature was capable of making such a striking noise. *Is it a call for help? Is it calling for me?*

A tear trickled down Adnil's cheek. She desperately wanted to see her offspring again, but knew she never would. Her chest ached, like a fresh open wound, as she agonized over the abrupt loss. The floodgates opened in an unfamiliar response, and she broke into uncontrollable sobbing. The sound of suffering echoed throughout the medical room, almost matching the intensity of the cries on the other side of the curtain. Adnil gasped for air in between the sobs. She had not had this reaction during previous extractions—the creature was just an object being removed from her body—but this time felt different. *Maybe it's because this time I kept my eyes open and watched the extraction,* reasoned Adnil. *Maybe it's all the talk about freedom and living in the outside world. If the creature had come out after we gained freedom, it would be mine to keep.*

Adnil agonized over this for some time until the combination of fatigue and drowsiness caused her to doze off. She tried to roll over, but her wrist was still locked down and her feet were still secured in the stirrups, making it impossible to shift position.

Adnil drifted in and out of sleep. She wanted to throw up each time she woke, when the memory of her heart-breaking experience mercilessly reappeared. The return to sleep was a welcome escape from her misery.

Through tired eyes, Adnil saw the blue uniform in front of her again as the commander conducted a series of probes. *The extraction is over. What's it looking for?* Next, Adnil felt her body being manhandled as some of her breast milk was drawn out with a hand-held pump. *Is the milk for my baby?* Once it finished with its tasks, the commander released her feet from the stirrups, but her wrist remained locked in the clamp.

Then the commander was gone again, leaving Adnil alone in quiet misery. The cold, hard examination table under her back made her shiver. She wished she was with Sky in their bunk. *How long will I have to lie here?*

She did not recall having to wait this long after previous extractions. Adnil wondered if the commander had forgotten about her. If that were the case, she might be stuck in this medical room for a long time. It was common not to see a commander in the compound for days. *I could die here.*

Time seemed to stand still in the windowless room; Adnil didn't know if it was day or night. After what felt like an eternity, the commander returned. Adnil's body welcomed the freedom of mobility as her wrist was released. As she was pushed back through the door into the familiar compound, she was greeted by a wall of heat.

Sky welcomed Adnil with a warm hug. "I was worried about you. How do you feel?"

"I gave birth to a baby," responded Adnil quietly. "It has dark hair like mine. I saw its small arms move. I saw its dark, shiny eyes and chubby cheeks. It has a little crescent moon on its forehead, and I will always remember it. Its name is Luna, and I am its mother."

CHAPTER 13

Joy sat on a small bench holding a chubby blond toddler on her knee while the rest of the girls sat on the floor in front of her. Joy smiled, taking pleasure in hearing the youthful voices sing with such exuberance.

> Twinkle, Twinkle, Little Star,
> How I wonder what you are.
> Up above the world so high.
> Like a diamond in the sky.
> Twinkle, Twinkle, Little Star,
> How I wonder what you are.

Joy did not know if other caregivers sang with the girls they supervised, or if they even cared about the children's quality of life. Flashbacks of her own free childhood were full of activities: playing outdoors, swimming, riding her bike, and ice skating. Joy remembered her dad was a good storyteller, adding much flare to his presentation. He could make even mundane prose sound fascinating.

If caring for the children was going to be her new role, she vowed she would give the girls the best life possible, considering the circumstances. *I'll work with what we have.* Joy sighed as she looked around the compound.

Most of the children's faces beamed as they sang the second verse, but some remained unreachable, like a snail hiding in its protective shell.

> When the blazing sun is gone,
> When it nothing shines upon.
> Then you show your little light.
> Twinkle, Twinkle, all the night.

Joy looked up as the door to the compound opened and a toddler was pushed through. It happened so fast that Joy only caught a glimpse of the commander's long alien fingers as they retreated to the outside world. The door shut, leaving the toddler to her unfortunate fate. She stood motionless, blue orphan eyes staring straight ahead, unfazed but expressionless.

Without missing a beat, Joy scooped the child up and was back at the bench before the second verse ended. The other children kept singing, indifferent to the thing that entered their quarters.

> Twinkle, Twinkle, Little Star,
> How I wonder what you are.

Toddlers arrived deprived of affection and lacking sensory stimulation. It took a lot of time and effort for Joy to draw out emotion from a young child's melancholic soul. Despite her resolute efforts, some children were only ever capable of showing artificial emotion, and others no emotion at all. Joy assumed that babies were kept in a different compound while they needed more comprehensive care, then transferred to this compound when they were toddlers.

Joy made it her goal to provide the girls with a variety of activities. Their days were full: immersed in stories, songs, play, imagination, and exploring. The physical environment limited the type of exploring they could do, but at least they had the yard. The children could explore dirt, stones, insects, puddles, and the boundless sky with its ever-changing visual stimulus.

Joy crafted small toys from scraps and sticks that blew over the wall. She organized a competitive game, similar to Valda and Dawn's stone toss, with the children. And she set a routine.

Joy knew routine gave children a sense of security and stability, so she divided up the day into defined sections. After the morning meal, the children had time for free play—the children could choose to play inside or outside regardless of the weather. In the middle of the day, when the sun was at its highest, she gathered the children inside for a singing session, followed by nap time. After nap time she led organized games and activities until the evening meal, following which they gathered for story time until it was time for bed.

Possessing a vibrant imagination, Joy had a talent for telling fantastical stories, inventing compelling imaginary worlds full of mythical characters. The worlds included wizards, fairies, nymphs, elves, and small animals, and the stories were laden with magic and epic adventures. The children's favourite story was one about a character named Skookum who lived on the planet Vandora. Skookum had powerful legs, enabling her to leap from the ground to the sky and land on top of a cloud. Then she would jump from cloud to cloud. Skookum had to be selective about the days she jumped, because if it started to rain when she was standing on a cloud, she would dissolve into the rain and fall back down to the ground. So Skookum only cloud-jumped when they were white and fluffy and stayed on the ground when they were dark and it looked like rain. The younger children listened with amusement and spent copious amounts of time entertaining themselves in the yard, assessing the clouds to determine whether it would be a good day for Skookum to jump.

Another story contained details about Earth, although the children did not know the setting was real, or that this world actually existed right outside the compound. To them, the mythical world in the story—including trees and streams, roads and houses, children and adults, and all kinds of intriguing food—was just as fantastical as Skookum's world.

Joy urged the children to create their own stories, encouraging them to use their imagination and expand their world beyond the boundaries of the compound. By doing so they learned to create an alternate world, which they could control and escape to when the burden they were bred for presented itself.

Joy did not disclose that they were locked inside a compound within a broader world. From their perspective, their entire world consisted of the compound and the adjoining yard. However, curiosity sometimes prompted questions from the older girls, and Joy always answered truthfully. Once the younger ones were tucked in their bunks for the night, Joy had conversations in the yard with the older children.

"What is on the other side of the wall?" they would ask. "And how come we never go out there?"

Joy struggled with keeping the right balance between truth-telling and making them feel safe. *Should I tell them their fate?*

What difference will it make? How do I prepare someone for a lifetime of despair and misery?

The bellies of two of the oldest girls were starting to grow. Joy knew their wretched lives would soon become even more miserable. Yet the parturient youngsters had no idea what was about to unfold, and she did not tell them unless they asked.

Joy hoped humans would find freedom and reclaim body sovereignty before too many more girls' bellies grew large and they were taken for their first extraction. It distressed her, like a stone in the heel of one's shoe on a long journey.

"How come the sky is black at night?" asked a curious preteen, one night out in the yard.

Joy cherished these moments, looking up in wonder at the night sky. "It looks black because at night we are facing away from the sun, our light source."

"How come the moon changes shape?" asked another child.

Joy badly wanted to tell all the children that the moon doesn't actually change shape—it only looked different because they only saw the parts lit by the sun as the moon orbited Earth—but it was difficult to give that kind of answer without first revealing that they were on a planet, suspended in a vast universe teeming with other planets. She longed to tell them about the great world beyond their artificial one.

Joy was comforted by the thought that at the very moment she was looking up at the moon, there was a strong possibility that Adnil was as well.

In the evening, when the children were asleep and she was alone in her bunk, Joy would lie awake thinking. Although she loved being with the children, she longed for adult companionship and for the day to arrive when they would all live together freely. At times in her loneliness, she would second guess herself and wonder if she was wrong in believing that they would be set free. *Am I mistakenly hopeful, waiting in vain for a day that will never come?*

CHAPTER 14

Adnil paced beside the wall, her mind churning as furiously as her legs, thinking about Joy's promise of release. Looking up to see the cat hop from the wall to the roof did nothing to quiet her thoughts: *When?* Seeing Valda drawing figures in the dirt with a stick, she asked the question out loud: "When will the commanders release us?"

"It's not going to happen that way," said Valda. "We can't just sit around waiting to be set free; that day may never come during our lifetime." The warm sun shone on Valda's determined face, spotlighting the burgeoning desire of a revolutionist.

"What makes you think that?" asked Adnil.

"Well anything is possible, but we can't wait around for change to happen. We have to *make* it happen." Valda continued drawing without looking up.

"But how? We are locked in here and don't have any control."

Valda looked up, eyes more serious and intent than Adnil had ever seen. "Me and Dawn got some ideas," she said in a quiet voice.

"I knew you guys were scheming something."

"When we spend time playing games in the yard, we're not always discussing the game you know..."

Valda suddenly rose, standing tall, facing Adnil with earnest eyes. "Are you in?" she asked, like a guerrilla leader signing up recruits.

"What do you mean?"

"What I mean is, are you going to help us? Do you want to be part of the team that works on a plan to set us free?"

Adnil admired Valda's courage and determination. She had Joy's hope for a positive future, but unlike Joy, she was willing to take matters into her own hands and orchestrate the change. Adnil looked up at the high wall that kept them confined. She thought of all who had been taken away from her, including Joy and Luna. "Yes, count me in."

Over the next few days, Valda collected a group of about ten women to start putting together ideas for the escape plan. They decided to keep the initial planning to this smaller group, with the intention of sharing it with the rest of the women once the plan was solidified. The group gathered in the yard.

"I think we should just refuse to go to the milking stations," suggested Aaron, excited to be part of an organized resistance. "Eventually they will give up and release us."

"That won't work," said Valda. "If hunger doesn't break us first, the commanders will eventually drag us over to the milking stations. You think we have it bad now? At least we have the freedom to walk around. If we refuse to go to the milking stations, that clamp holding our arm in place during milking will never be released. They will just leave us there and we will have to shit, eat, sleep, and be milked from that position for our entire lives."

The women grimaced in horror at the image Valda described. It provided great incentive to come up with a foolproof method of escape.

"How about we climb up and over the wall?" suggested Adnil, pointing.

Dawn replied, "We haven't figured out how to scale the wall. Besides, even if we found a way to do it, it would take too long to get everybody over it, and some of the women with big bellies might have a difficult time. The wall's just way too high."

"How about we dig a tunnel under the wall?" was the next suggestion.

"There are too many unknowns with a tunnel," said Robin. "What direction would we dig? How far forward would we have to dig before we started digging up to the surface? We don't even know what's on the other side of the wall. We might end up digging a tunnel that leads into another locked compound."

"Or our tunnel might lead into the commander's living area and we catch them on the toilet," said Dawn, causing the women to laugh.

"We only have one chance, and it has to be successful," said Valda, guiding the conversation back to reality. "If we fail, they will be on to us, and our lives will never be the same. We will be permanently locked down, you can be sure. I think we need to physically overpower a commander. We tackle the asshole into submission and restrain it. Then we use its wristband to scan the reader, unlock the door and walk out with our heads held high."

"That's clever," said Dawn. "I like that plan."

"Okay, but what happens if we run into more Xplerians on the other side of the door?" asked Robin.

Adnil thought how beneficial it was to have Robin in the planning group, scrutinizing the plan from all angles as it was developing.

"Then we will have to kill them," responded Valda with a look of determination.

It was as if Valda had been waiting for this moment her entire life. She was committed to reclaiming freedom for the women. She was willing to fight for it, even if it included a physical altercation with a commander and the challenge of an unknown environment once they exited the compound doors. After much debate, the women agreed and supported Valda's idea.

"Now we have to come up with a game plan. We need to figure out *how* this will happen, *when* this will happen, and what preparation is required." Valda spoke with the confidence of a natural organizer.

Except for the role of teacher, there was no hierarchy among the women; they had never required one. But now, with their first-ever goal, they were instinctively aware that they needed a team leader. Without discussion, Valda assumed the role of coordinating the escape plan. The rest of the team complied, happy to have someone in charge who was both willing and capable of taking on the task.

"Dawn will be responsible for stockpiling weapons," said Valda.

"Where the heck will we get weapons?" said Aaron.

"We started collecting them some time ago," said Dawn proudly. "We've been stealing items that could double as weapons from the medical room. It's best to steal them over time, so the commanders don't notice. And to mess with them, we steal more when we notice a change in commanders. That way they can blame the newbie for the missing items," she added with a smirk on her face.

The group met in the yard every day after the morning education session. Together, they started fashioning a rough timeline and course of action.

"When is the best time to execute the escape?" Valda asked them.

The sooner the better, thought Adnil as she gazed at the wall.

"Timing is important." Valda answered her own question. "It would be better to do it when only *one* commander enters the compound. It will be easier to physically take one down."

The women all agreed on that. Although a commander most often entered the compound towards the end of a milking session, the group determined that this would be a terrible time to execute the escape plan.

"We all finish milking at different times," said Valda. "We can't have some of us still locked in place while the others are trying to tackle the commander to the ground. It would be better to do it when nobody is locked down."

"You're right," responded Robin. "Although it doesn't happen as frequently, we need to be patient and wait for *one* commander to enter *outside* of milking time."

The women nodded and voiced their agreement. Adnil thought how nice it was to experience this collaboration among the women. She thought of how proud Joy would have been to witness these bright minds constructing an important plan of action in harmony.

Adnil stretched out in the bunk, still thinking about the earlier planning meeting. With Sky in the yard, she extended her body to fill the bunk and gave a satisfying yawn. Planning for the future was both energizing and exhausting at the same time, and she felt more hopeful and excited about the future than ever before.

On waking from a brief nap, Adnil went searching for Sky. There was more activity than usual in the yard, and she sensed positive energy in the air. She found Sky playing a target game with Aaron and Dawn. Adnil had never really enjoyed taking part in games before, but somehow she felt different today and joined them. There was a bond growing amongst the planning group, brought on by the possibility of a brighter future and the challenge of working together to attain it. They played a boisterous game until the bell rang. As they walked towards the entrance to the compound, Adnil wondered how many more times in their lives they would be summoned by that bell.

CHAPTER 15

Valda sized up the group, looking uncertain. "The next decision to make is which of us will have the honour of tackling the commander into submission."

"Why don't we all gang up on the schmuck at once?" said Aaron.

"It might be better to limit this job to a small unit of capable fighters," said Valda, like a seasoned general. "Otherwise we'll just be an ineffective mob of misfits."

The women looked at each other sheepishly to see if there were any gutsy volunteers longing for a wrangle with a commander, but no one stepped forward. Then suggestions erupted like a freak hail storm during a summer heatwave.

"It should be the strongest ones."

"It should include someone who is fast on their feet."

"We need someone with a fierce attitude."

Still no one stepped forward to volunteer, nor was anyone nominated. After more discussion, the group realized it was premature to select enforcers without first discovering what each of them was capable of. Not having participated in feats of strength before, they had no way of knowing.

"We gotta experiment to find out which combat manoeuvres work the best," said Valda. "Once we figure that out, we can practice on each other and see who is the most skilled."

Next on the agenda was determining how to use the commander's wristband to open the door leading to their freedom. "Once we restrain the asshole, we'll remove the wristband," said Dawn. "We've got some sharp tools in our collection that we can use to cut it off."

"Once two designated fighters overpower the commander, two others can work on cutting the band off its wrist," suggested Valda. "Then we simply unlock the door and walk out of this prison."

The women cheered loudly and enthusiastically.

The discussion moved to supplies. "I think every person should keep a sharp tool or knife on them," said Valda. "We might need it for self defence once we're outside."

"I agree," said Robin. "Besides acting as a weapon, it can be used for digging or for cutting edible plants." She remembered many foraging adventures with her friends, scavenging for wild edibles. Back then, it was a hobby. Little did she know that one day she would be foraging for wild food out of necessity.

"Right now, we don't have enough sharps for everyone, so we will have to steal a lot more," said Dawn.

"That could take too long, and it might bring unwelcome attention if we steal too many at once," said Valda. "The last thing we need right now is another search of our quarters."

"Why don't we make more by sharpening stones we find in the yard," suggested Adnil.

"That's worth a try," said Valda.

"Once we are outside the compound, each person will need to remove their own wristband with their tool," said Robin. "Just in case the band has a tracking device in it, it will be best to remove it right away."

The women formed committees, assigning themselves roles and responsibilities. Dawn, who was in charge of expanding the weapon supply, selected a few others to help sharpen stones.

"It will be important to take along water," said Robin at the next planning meeting. "We won't last long without it, especially in this heat."

"Won't we be able to find water in the outside world?" said Adnil.

"Hopefully, but there's no guarantee; this is the dry season," said Robin. "Even if water sources are available, they might be hard to locate."

"Too bad we don't have containers to fill with water to carry with us," said Aaron.

"Wait. I think I have just the thing." Dawn quickly ran inside, returning moments later. "You mean something like this?" She pulled a small bottle out of her tunic.

"How did you get that?" said Aaron.

"This is part of my stash," said Dawn.

"During our escape, we can get more. There are loads of bottles in the medical room," said Adnil, remembering the sight of them during her last visit.

"They will have to be rinsed really well," said Robin. "It would be disastrous to die from drinking poison right after our escape. I volunteer to empty and refill the bottles on escape day," she said, realizing she was the only one remotely capable of surmising the contents of each bottle.

Sky, who was in charge of figuring out the best way to carry supplies, discovered by trial and error that a blanket could be folded and wrapped around the body to serve as a backpack. This would enable them to remain hands-free and unencumbered while on the move. A blanket folding drill was repeated over and over during practice sessions. Although it was not a difficult skill to master, learning to do it quickly under pressure was vital. Races were held to see who could assemble their backpack the fastest.

The women gathered whatever they could find that seemed useful, aiming for each to carry one extra blanket, any tool or weapon they had, and a bottle of water. Everything else they owned they were wearing.

The backpacks serendipitously revealed the benefits of wrapping material tightly around the body, and subsequently makeshift supportive bras—referred to as warrior-wear—were designed from strips of thin blanket as well.

Revealing the plan to the entire group was a momentous step. The announcement caused a flurry of excitement, but sober reality followed as the seriousness of the precarious undertaking sank in.

"In order to have a remote chance of success," said Robin, "everyone must be on board with the plan, and everyone must be committed to putting in the work to make it happen. That means endless drills and lots of rigorous physical practice."

"We are committed! We are ready," the group responded without hesitation.

With everyone eager to move the plan forward, Valda gathered the women in the yard to dream up combat manoeuvres. A spotter stood guard in the doorway ready to warn of a commander entering, which would instantly pause all activity.

They experimented with different techniques, first awkwardly, then more proficiently as they gradually grew accustomed to the physical combat.

"Okay, I need two volunteers to try a practice fight," said Valda on the first day of scrimmaging.

Nobody stepped forward, each too timid to enter the boxing ring.

"Shake a leg and start moving, people!" said Valda. "If nobody steps forward, I'll pick someone. We all have to try it eventually, so snap to it!"

Two reluctant fighters stepped forward, ready for a sparring match, while the others formed a circle around them, shouting suggestions and encouragement. The two novice fighters stood face to face in ready position, knees bent and feet firmly planted on the ground, shoulder-width apart.

Movement replaced fixed footing as the hesitant fighters circled, eyeing each other nervously, each waiting for the right moment to pounce on their adversary.

"Try to picture a commander in front of you," suggested Valda. "It's payback time!"

"Grab her by the throat," yelled Adnil, surprised by the sudden outburst. Her heart was racing with excitement as she experienced her very first adrenaline rush. The sparring partners continued to dance around each other, moving in cautious circles while awkwardly trying to grab their opponent's arms in an effort to pull them to the ground. The technique was not very successful, and they bobbed forward and then retreated like a pair of competing crows alternately picking at roadkill.

"Try to distract your opponent first, with a hit or kick, before tackling them," suggested Valda. The two fighters followed this recommendation and experimented by delivering sloppy, slow swings. Some of the swings landed gently on their opponent's shoulder, stomach, and legs, but others were merely air punches. The novice fighters were as timid about hitting their opponent as they were about getting hit.

Once the first fighters were too spent to continue sparring, Valda eyed the yard for two more participants. "How about Adnil and Aaron?"

Adnil's stomach felt queasy. Overcoming the uneasiness, she timidly stepped forward into the circle to face her opponent. "This isn't quite a fair match," she protested. "My opponent is much taller than me."

"Well, Xplerians are much taller than humans, so you better get used to it," Robin said.

Adnil faced her towering opponent, hoping nobody noticed her shaking legs. The two combatants faced each other, fists in front of their faces ready to both protect themselves and possibly deliver a blow. Their eyes locked as they sized each other up. Adnil was the first one to receive a hit, with a soft punch landing on her right shoulder. Moments later, she was struck again, this time on the left shoulder. *Ouch!* The second hit was a little harder. While Adnil was trying to determine precisely how to position her hands, a third hit landed on her. The hard thud caught her off guard and knocked her back.

Adnil's body, impatient with her cognitive analysis of appropriate hand placement, decided it was time to act on its own. Impulsively pulling her arm back to wind up, she stepped forward and forcefully thrust the heel of her hand upward, making solid contact right under Aaron's nose.

Adnil's sucker-punch sent her tall opponent flying, knocking her to the ground—and out cold. There was blood everywhere. Chaos erupted like a volcanic explosion. People scattered, someone rushed inside to get a blanket and soaked it in the water fountain on the way back. Others crowded around to see if the victim was still alive. The first-responder wiping blood off Aaron's face with the wet blanket was relieved to see the patient open her eyes.

"I—I think ... my nose ... is broken!" said Aaron, as she came to.

"Keep her lying down and elevate her legs," said Robin, as her medical training kicked in. She placed her index and middle fingers on the side of Aaron's neck. "Her pulse rate seems okay."

"We better stop for today," said Valda. "I'm sorry that someone got hurt, but the good news is we discovered a technique that works incredibly well."

#

"That was quite a fight you had, Adnil," said Robin later in the yard under the night sky. "Everyone is talking about it. They are referring to your technique as the *Adnil power punch.*"

"I am so sorry. I feel bad for Aaron."

"I feel bad for her too, but don't be sorry about it," said Robin. "You didn't know what the result would be. Physical fighting is new to us and we are just experimenting. Remember, everything we discover during our training can be used against a commander later. The training is important. It is our ticket out of here."

"I feel bad about something else though," said Adnil, hoping she could confide in Robin. She looked her friend straight in the eye, hoping what she was about to say wouldn't make Robin think less of her. "It felt good. It felt good to hit someone and hurt them. It felt *really* good."

Robin looked at Adnil with understanding. "There's a chance that you might be confusing your emotions, Adnil. Perhaps you felt good because that action made you feel powerful. It made you feel like you could defend yourself. Being in confinement makes us feel powerless, and for the first time, you had a taste of being powerful and in control."

Adnil was reassured by Robin's interpretation. It was better than her own assumption that she possessed an innate desire to inflict pain on others.

When the women gathered again the next day to practice fighting, they were very reluctant to hit each other.

"I don't want to volunteer to get smashed in the face," said Dawn, after Valda suggested she be the next one to spar.

"And I'm not interested in giving anyone a bloody nose," said Aaron, knowing what it was like to be at the receiving end.

Adnil kept quiet and avoided eye contact with others, remembering what Robin had said about how the infamous Adnil power punch contributed greatly to the end goal.

"It's understandable that you are timid considering what happened in our first training session," said Valda. "However, remember that it is important for us to develop the skills so we can overpower a commander. Keep that in mind. For now, we will tone it down. Fight in slow motion, simulating actions using soft hits instead of actually going through with full force."

The women murmured, mulling over Valda's suggestion, and eventually agreed it was a sensible solution.

"Good. Now, divide up in pairs and practise that way," said Valda. "Chop! Chop! Let's get moving, people." Appeased with the modification, the group happily cooperated and began coupling up to start their second combat training session.

"Oh, and I was thinking about our fist punches," added Valda. "The punches might be more deadly if you make a slight change. Instead of holding a closed flat fist with all the fingers lined up evenly, keep the knuckle of the middle finger sticking out a bit. Test it out using very light punches against each other's arms.

"It is as different as night and day," said Robin, after giving it a try. "Valda, that is remarkable. It turns a regular fist into an enhanced weapon."

"This hit will knock the commander off its feet," added Dawn.

Valda grinned, pleased with the useful discovery.

The group practised various striking techniques before switching to wrestling.

"I am stuck. I give up," said Sky, as Dawn held her in a tight headlock. "Let me go, please."

"Do you think the commander is going to let you go if you ask nicely?" yelled Valda. "Come on Sky, try to find a way to get yourself free. Be resourceful."

Sky continued squirming, struggling to release herself from the tight hold before changing tactics.

"Ouch!" screamed Dawn, abandoning the hold. "She bit me!" She examined the wound.

"I was told to be resourceful," responded Sky in defence.

"Good job, Sky," said Valda. "You got the result you were aiming for. Another option would have been to use an elbow jab. The elbow is quite sharp—especially yours, Sky. If the commander has a tight grip on you, strike it in the stomach with your elbow."

The women continued practising until the bell summoned them to their stations.

CHAPTER 16

There was no going back. They were done with enslavement. They were going to leave the compound or die trying. Although the group had put a lot of effort into planning their escape, their journey beyond it was less defined. It was impossible to know exactly what to expect once they exited the door of the compound. All they could do was arm themselves with survival skills for what they imagined might lie ahead.

Adnil was in charge of improving general physical conditioning. In order to increase their chance of survival after the escape, they had to be in good physical condition. They needed to be able to sprint short distances, but also needed endurance for travelling long distances. They needed strength for running, climbing, and possibly fighting Xplerians. The confined space they had spent a lifetime in had limitations as a training facility, so Adnil had to get creative. She directed her trainees to run around the perimeter of the yard for as long as possible. It wasn't an ideal running track, but it was all they had. After years of the sedentary lifestyle of a milker, the women fatigued easily during the initial training.

"Why do we have to run around so many times? It's too hot," complained Sky. "Isn't it my turn to be on guard for commanders today?"

"Just snap to it and get moving. Chop! Chop!" said Valda, having overheard the complaint as she ran past Sky.

"You too, Simone," said Valda in a somewhat softer voice, as she ran past a milker with a growing belly who had slowed down to a fast walk.

"If you are being chased by an Xplerian, who do you want the superior runner to be?" asked Adnil. "Remember, they have longer legs than humans, so they have an advantage. Having a superior fitness level will be *our* advantage." Adnil's prodding paid off and gradually they were able to substantially increase the distance they could run.

Adnil also introduced bursts of short-distance running, making the women sprint back and forth from wall to wall at top speed. To make it more interesting, Adnil divided them into teams and had them compete in relay races. When the novelty wore off, she increased the challenge and intensity with hurdles—humans positioned on their hands and knees—to leap over at full speed.

One team was particularly adept at jumping hurdles and bragged about it. "I think it would be nearly impossible to beat our team," said Aaron, knowing that her long legs made her particularly skilled at the activity.

"Yes, we are no doubt the best team at jumping hurdles," agreed one of her teammates.

Finally, a member of the opposing team found a way to curb the gloating. Just as a particularly boastful runner jumped, the hurdle arched her back high in the air, like a cat stretching sleepy muscles after a nap. The surprise impact sent the runner flying and triggered an outright brawl between the two teams. Even Robin was in on it. Fire raged through her veins as she fought with fury. Fists flew, legs kicked, and bodies rolled. People were actually getting hurt.

"It's mayhem out there!" said Valda.

"Aren't you going to break it up?" Sky asked Adnil, who stood on the sidelines, watching.

"How do I do that?" replied Adnil. "Besides, maybe this is good practice. Maybe we *need* to be a little angry."

"Yeah, but not at each other," said Sky.

The skirmish eventually petered out, leaving battle-fatigued, sweaty bodies strewn all over the yard. Robin lay breathless on the ground, processing what just happened, especially her participation in the crazed frenzy. Her right eye was starting to swell where she had received a punch. She slowly picked herself up and walked over to Adnil, feeling the need to give some kind of explanation for her unorthodox behaviour.

"I-I don't normally condone violent outbursts … and disorderly behaviour," said Robin, "but … for the greater cause—"

"Yeah, yeah, yeah," interrupted Valda. "Fess up Robin, did you lose control?"

Robin smiled, shrugging her shoulders in silence. It wasn't like her to lose control. Robin's sheepish eyes met Adnil's, searching for her reaction. Adnil chuckled with understanding. *After all, my own loss of control resulted in the invention of the Adnil power punch.*

Despite the dramatic turn of events, the spontaneous brawl was a good way to wrap up the afternoon drills. Adrenaline rushes were new to them, and they relished the exhilaration as fire coursed through their veins, leaving them wanting more.

Evening singing sessions were now replaced with competitions involving feats of strength. Some wrestling and push-up contests lasted well into the wee hours of the morning, when one person defeated all rivals and was declared the winner. The competitive nature, which had been non-existent in the past, intensified into a healthy rivalry. The chance to be declared a champion was just as much of a motivator as the long-term goal of escape. Once labelled a champion, the winner would fiercely defend the title during subsequent contests.

Eventually, the two most skilled fighters—Aaron and Beth—were selected to tackle the commander into submission. A second tier of fighters was designated as backups.

"I think we need a third team on standby," said Valda. "Just in case the first two tiers of fighters are, you know, defeated."

"What do you mean 'defeated'?" asked Aaron. "Do you think we're not capable of victory?"

"I just think we need a plan that is fail-proof," said Valda. "We need a strong offence, and it can't hurt to have a third team of fighters ready to step in."

"I agree," said Robin. "We have no idea how strong a commander is. They are not human, and we won't know how much effort it will take to bring one down until it actually happens."

And so it was agreed that having a third tier of fighters on standby would be good insurance. Throughout the fall and winter seasons, they all practiced.

"I think the physical training you are putting us through is really working," said Sky to Adnil one evening in the yard. "I feel a lot stronger."

"Good," said Adnil. "We need our strength. Freedom is almost within reach."

"What do you want out of your life if we ever leave here?" said Sky.

"You mean *when* we leave here."

"Yes, *when* we leave here."

"It's so hard to say," said Adnil. "All I've ever done is exist. There were no plans until we created the escape plan. We won't know what is even possible until we get out."

"It will be kinda scary, but I am glad we can go through it together," said Sky. "We can support each other, right, Adnil?"

"Yes, I promise you that," said Adnil, pulling Sky in close.

CHAPTER 17

Robin now focussed the education sessions on practical knowledge, which would be needed for survival in what she expected would be a rural area—although no one really knew what they would find when they walked out the compound door.

About a year into captivity, Robin accepted that the enslavement could last generations. So she consciously recalled bits of information in an effort to solidly store them in her memory, like backing up computer data. Her only worry was that the information might not be relevant by the time they got out, remembering how everything used to change so rapidly that the average person sometimes struggled to stay current. But her outdated memory bank was all the women had. The responsibility of being the only surviving original weighed heavily on her.

Robin looked out at the eager faces hanging on her every word now that the information she shared had a practical application. She let out a deep breath. She hoped she wouldn't forget vital information that would be useful to their survival.

"You need to be mentally prepared," said Robin. "Life in the compound has been predictable. Life in the outside world will be the opposite." Robin decided to start with general instructions, then add details as time permitted. After all, they couldn't predict when their opportunity for escape would arise.

"Once outside, move west. West is the direction the sun travels across the sky. We will likely walk through fields, then through forests, and if we go far enough, we will reach the ocean. I expect it will take us three to four days, depending on how fast we walk."

"How do you know the ocean is nearby?" asked Adnil.

"You can smell a hint of ocean in the air on days when a strong wind blows from the west," replied Robin, as if stating the obvious.

"What's an ocean?" asked a recent arrival who had not been to many education sessions.

"We'll talk about the ocean in more detail later," Robin said after giving a brief description for the benefit of the newcomer. "Our compound is within a region that was known as Cascadia," Robin continued. "Originally, the region was covered in coastal rainforests teeming with trees. Immediately before colonization, many forests had large sections of trees missing due to—"

"Um … what are trees?" said Sky, knowing that she was speaking for many in the group.

Good point. Past education sessions had covered astronomy, zoology, meteorology, and occasionally bits of ancient poetry, but never basic botany.

Robin paused, deliberating how to best answer the question. Describing trees to people who rarely saw any plants was like describing an object to a blind person, but without the benefit of touch and smell as well.

"Imagine a person standing upright, with their legs joined together as one, and arms raised. Only instead of two arms, they have multiple arms reaching out in all directions. The arms are called branches and the branches have smaller branches extending from them. At the end of each branch, there are green leaves growing. Think of the leaves as green hair."

"What! Trees are green, like our tunics?" said Dawn. "I was imagining them to have brighter colours like pink or red."

"The base of the tree is brown, like the dirt on the ground in the yard. The outer skin on the base is thick and rough. And yes, the leaves of the tree are green like our tunics." said Robin. "Trees are majestic life forms. My words cannot adequately describe the awe you will feel when you see a stately, mature cedar tree for the first time." She remembered how she felt walking through some of the region's last remaining old-growth forests many years ago.

"Follow me. I think there's an image on the wall." Robin led them out to the yard to look at a small petroglyph etched by one of the originals.

"Cedars are a special type of tree that keeps its green hair all the time." Robin continued with the description. "Full-grown trees are much wider and taller than you and me."

"As tall as the commanders?" asked Simone.

"Mature ones are even taller than those walls," Robin said, pointing up. "Some can even be three times as tall." She remembered the cedars she had seen on hikes with friends.

"The tree is a living thing that eats and breathes," continued Robin.

"What do they eat?" asked Adnil.

"They don't have mouths like we do," said Robin. "Instead, they have many hoses on the bottom of their feet that travel into the ground and suck up food from below the earth. The food then turns to sap, which is similar to our blood, and runs up and down the tree to spread the nutrition to the entire body of the tree."

"Do trees live together, or do they live alone?" said Adnil.

"If left alone, without human interference, trees will naturally grow in communities called forests," said Robin. "They look out for each other. They are connected below the ground. There's a nutrient network beneath old trees that helps members of the forests share food. The mother trees communicate and are programmed to protect younger ones."

"Some types of trees, less common to this region, change colours," explained Robin. "They have flat leaves instead of scaly leaves, and when the weather starts getting colder, the leaves turn from green to red, orange, or yellow. Then the leaves drop off and the trees are bare."

"Bare?" said Dawn. "You mean they lose their hair and become bald like the commanders?"

"Yes, but the leaves grow back again when the cold season is over," said Robin, remembering the circle of life witnessed in the changing season.

Robin continued talking as they moved back to their stools inside. "Just like with mammals, there are many different species of trees. The types of trees in this region before colonization were mainly cedar and fir, similar to the picture drawn on the wall. However, in the most recent years before colonization, the climate was changing and the forest in this area was becoming drier. Species such as redwoods and sequoias that were accustomed to drier climates were starting to creep northward from the drier south."

"What is a climate?" asked Sky.

Too much information. Robin realized she had to limit the facts to just what they needed to know for survival. "It's just a fancy name for weather. When we leave this compound, the forest can provide food, but you will have to know what to look for and how to gather it."

"Won't there be food dispensers along the way?" Simone asked half-jokingly, but with serious concern about how she was going to find food.

Robin took a deep breath. "The enriched food we get here four times a day will not be available. What we get in here is processed food, specially designed for milkers. The wild food you will be looking for is quite different, and you will have to work hard to find it at first."

"It will be a welcome change to choose our own food," said Dawn. "I am tired of eating the mush they feed us."

"Choose?" Robin frowned at the overconfident reaction of expecting a smorgasbord. "This might not sound believable inside these walls, but there might be a time in the early days of our escape that you miss this food terribly. Finding our own food can be a challenge. Wild animals spend most of their time searching for food. When you first become wild, you will do the same."

"Well, I am up for the challenge," said Valda. "I wanna be wild, even if it requires a little competition for food."

"You will find edible plants growing in the ground," said Robin. "I hope we escape before the cold season starts, so we have more options." She looked blankly into the air, absently tugging at her uniform.

"Food grows naturally in the wild." Robin refocussed her attention on the group. "But it can also be intentionally planted and harvested, which I think is what the Xplerians do to make our food. Cultivated food is typically grown in large plots of land and appears unnaturally uniform, meaning it is the only type of plant in that section. There's a chance we will walk right by the plants the Xplerians grow to make our food."

"Before humans began mass-producing food, they relied on foraging to eat," said Robin. "Foraging can be rewarding, but one requires a little knowledge to be good at it. You will come across edible berries like raspberries, blueberries, salal, saskatoon, and salmonberries."

Robin described what each berry looked like and where to find it. "The forest floor also has native plants such as kinnikinnick, lupin, and fern," continued Robin, explaining more about each plant. "There are also edible mushrooms that grow on the forest floor," said Robin, remembering foraging for wild mushrooms as a hobby during days off with her co-workers from the Garden Centre.

In the yard, Robin used a stick to draw outlines of each type of mushroom in the dirt, pointing out the gills and different shapes and sizes of their caps and stem. "Common types in this region are chanterelles, lobster mushrooms, fall oyster mushrooms, porcini mushrooms, and pine mushrooms. But be aware of the poisonous ones. They can kill you."

"What?" said Dawn. "Some wild foods kill you? Who came up with that plan?"

Robin nodded. "Avoid mushrooms with red on the cap or stem, white gills, a ring on the stem, or a bulbous, sack-like base."

"Whoa! I will never remember this information and will end up dead for sure," said Sky. "I think only Robin should pick the mushrooms."

"It can be hard to determine which mushrooms are poisonous, so if you have enough other food and don't want to take a risk, just don't eat mushrooms," suggested Robin.

"There are also non-native plants such as blackberries," Robin continued. "We might find them outside the forest because they thrive in areas of full sun. Blackberries used to spread like crazy in this region." She could see the sprawling brambles covered with plump, deep-purple orbs in her mind.

"The plants produce sweet, juicy, tasty berries near the end of the warm season. Right about now," said Robin, getting caught up in the memory of long forgotten food. "Jeez, I really hope we come across them."

"What does sweet mean?" asked Adnil.

Robin racked her brain. *How do I describe a taste sensation to people whose tongue has only ever encountered mono-flavour?* "I can't describe *sweet*, but it will be a delightful surprise for your tongue when you bite into a blackberry," Robin finally said aloud.

"That sounds more like it," said Dawn. "I will stay away from poisonous mushrooms and eat blackberries."

"Beware when you try to pick them. The plant can grab hold of you," warned Robin.

"Grab us?" said Dawn. "I knew it was too good to be true. Another food type that wants to kill humans."

"They won't kill you, but they have small sharp thorns that will pierce into your skin or clothing, and not let go."

"In that case, why would anyone bother to try to pick blackberries?" asked Aaron.

"Because if you come across blackberry bushes, ripe with berries at a time when you are hungry, you will consider it a gift," said Robin. "When you come across them, you can either complain because blackberry bushes have thorns, or rejoice because thorn bushes have blackberries. I guess it will depend on how hungry you are."

"First you said some foods might kill us, and now you are saying other foods will attack us!" exclaimed Dawn. "I take back my comment about looking forward to being able to choose my own food. Why does it have to be so complicated?"

"Well there's even more to be cautious about," said Robin. "You might run into competition. You will not be the *only* animal foraging for food. If you encounter a bear, walk away from it. Don't fight it over rights to a blackberry patch, because you won't win. Those big, brown, furry animals are taller and stronger than you."

"Even when faced with an Adnil power punch?" said Valda with a smile.

"Let's just say it's not worth trying to find out the answer to that question," said Robin.

"Getting food in the outside world seems like a lot of work," muttered Sky, narrowing her eyes.

"It can be," replied Robin. "Dehydration is the real risk. We'll take along some water but will run out quickly. Finding fresh water, or at least juicy fruit, is absolutely essential to avoid dehydration. You can only last three days without water."

Robin paused, letting reality sink in.

"Living in the outside world will not always be pure bliss," she said. "Success will not come automatically. We will have good days and bad days. The price you pay for independence is high. It takes a lot of work to be responsible for your own survival. But the reward is a more meaningful, gratifying, and fulfilling life."

#

Adnil had listened carefully to the lesson and looked forward to being in the bizarre magical forest that Robin described. Adnil could relate to mother trees communicating, programmed to protect their young. Her heart ached as she remembered the urge to protect her young. Not the first two extracted creatures, but the one she actually looked at. The one with the crescent moon on its forehead. Luna. Adnil looked across the courtyard at Simone's large belly. She felt like warning her not to open her eyes during the upcoming extraction because once you see something, you can't unsee it.

I wonder what real food tastes and feels like, thought Adnil, trying to imagine something other than the familiar puree touching her tongue. The world Robin described felt very far away from her current life, yet it was right outside her door, and she would soon be walking in it. Robin had said it took a lot of work to be responsible for your own survival, but Adnil was not afraid. She wouldn't be alone. She was comforted by the fact that she was part of a community of individuals who had a shared history. And now they had a shared goal. They would look out for each other. They would pool their strength. If they stuck together, Adnil was confident they would make it.

CHAPTER 18

"How will the group know when it is time to launch the escape?" asked Adnil after one of the training sessions.

"One of us will need to make that call," said Valda. "When an ideal moment presents itself, they will have to make a quick decision and signal to everyone."

"It needs to be someone who is observant, confident, and unflinching," added Robin.

The group unanimously decided the best person was Valda.

"I accept," said Valda, undaunted by the responsibility. "Now we need to decide on a distinct signal."

"Why do we need a special signal?" asked Aaron. "Can't you just yell out instructions when it is time?"

"A unique signal is better, clearer than me yelling a bunch of instructions," said Valda.

"Good point," said Aaron. "You yell a lot normally, so we wouldn't necessarily be able to tell if it was escape time, or if it was just you being you."

Valda glared at Aaron.

"The signal should be short, unique, and require no explanation," said Robin before the argument could escalate.

"Once we hear the signal, we will immediately follow the plan of action that we've been rehearsing."

"We have to catch the commander off guard, a complete surprise," said Valda. "We don't want the asshole to see it coming. Once the signal is given, the execution needs to be fast and furious."

"I can't wait to see the expression on its face when the shit hits the fan," said Dawn, grinning from ear to ear.

"We'll go through training drills to practice the launch procedure. Everyone will know their specific role," said Robin.

"Okay, any ideas for a word or phrase for the launch signal?" asked Valda.

"It needs to be something we wouldn't regularly use," said Robin. "When it is shouted out, there cannot be any doubt or confusion. Any ideas?"

"Action?"

"Freedom Time?"

Several more ideas were suggested, but were rejected by the group. They were stumped.

"Our ideas suck. We'll talk about it another time," said Valda.

They switched topics for the remainder of the meeting. The next day, after the morning milking, the planning group reconvened in the yard under a sky that looked dark and ominous. A warm, dry wind swept through the yard, picking up dirt and dust and spinning it into a mini funnel that moved across the yard before losing energy and dying out.

"Hopefully we can finish our meeting before a storm comes," said Valda, after she cleared the dusty phlegm from her throat and spat on the ground. "Any ideas for the launch signal?"

"Time for Flowers to Bloom," suggested Simone, which was followed by a collective groan from the group.

"What's wrong with it?" said Simone, throwing her hands up in the air.

"It sounds stupid," replied Dawn. "In the future, when we are free, we will refer to this tactical operation that transformed our lives. It can't be lame. Besides, it's too long."

Motivated by the threat of having a weak moniker for the signal that would launch their monumental escape, the women dug deep to think of alternative ideas.

"We need a signal that has more energy," said Adnil, as another gust of dry wind swept through the yard.

The threat of the oncoming windstorm sparked their creativity.

"How about Freak Storm?" suggested Aaron.

"What about Lightning Strike?" suggested another.

A peal of thunder rolled across the sky, settling the discussion: Operation Thunder would be the signal.

The escape plan was rehearsed daily, but continuously improved. Although nervous, everyone was committed to Operation Thunder and worked hard to fine tune their path to freedom.

CHAPTER 19

The door to the compound opened, and a new arrival was pushed inside. She was older than the typical newcomer and walked with a limp. Even more striking to Adnil was the look of confidence and experience in her eyes rather than the usual expression of shock and fear.

"My name is Star." The self-assured arrival introduced herself while she circulated, getting familiar with her surroundings as if it were a regular occurrence. "It's a new name I recently gave myself to match da bright future ahead of me."

To Adnil, Star appeared to be knowledgeable and confident. At her previous compound, the commanders, who she referred to as farmers, were very talkative.

"I was always listening to dem and learned to understand some of da language," she said proudly. "It was something I mostly did cuz I was bored, but recently it became useful. I learned about da big changes dat are happening in da Xplerian world."

"Changes?" asked Robin, raising her brows.

"Yep, things are changing in da outside world, my friends. Da place I recently lived in wuz closed down."

With wide eyes, the women hung on every word coming from the mouth of this exotic arrival.

"A recall was made for da Xplerians to go back to da home planet," said Star.

"What?"

"Why?"

"I don't know, but I think it's cuz of finding rich resources on a different planet."

"So it's not because the Xplerians evolved to realize that exploiting humans for their own gain is morally wrong?" asked Valda sarcastically.

"Huh?" said Star, unsure what Valda was asking. "No, I am pretty sure it's cuz of da rich resources on a different planet."

Robin's jaw dropped at the news. "Are you saying the Xplerians are leaving Earth and we will soon be set free?"

Star shook her head. "I wish it was so. Dissent exists among da Xplerians. Many of dem are not obeying da directive to leave Earth. Some want to stay. I heard it was happening worldwide. Da ones dat are leaving, are selling da humans, or abandoning dem. Da ones dat are staying are still farming as usual. Some of dem are even trying to increase da herd size, buying human stock for a low price. I was sold, but I suspect da farmers did not get a good price for me. Da younger ones are worth more. Some farmers are going to abandoned farms to scoop up da humans dat were left behind. It is very chaotic at da moment."

With this new information, the women debated about whether they should go through with their escape plan.

"I think we should wait it out," said Aaron. "Maybe we will be set free soon."

"I don't think we can afford to wait," said Robin, looking towards Star for her reaction.

Details of the escape plan were shared with Star and she was asked whether they should go through with it considering the recent changes in the Xplerian community.

"Do not sit around and wait to be set free," said Star. "You have no guarantee you will be set free. In fact, if you don't get da blaze out of here now, worse things could happen to you."

"Worse than our current lives?" said Adnil.

"Yep, worse," said Star. "If your farmers decide to return to da home planet, you could be sold, or you could be abandoned and trapped in dis compound to slowly starve. Rebel farmers might come snooping 'round in search of some free humans. How do dem options sound to ya?"

Adnil's heart leapt to her throat. The look of horror on the other women's faces matched her fear.

"I think we need to stick to the original plan and take control of our own destiny," said Valda. Audible sighs of relief echoed through the compound.

Later, Adnil pondered the new information as she watched the sun drop below the top of the wall. Adnil imagined the sunsets she would see in a free world without the obstruction of a high wall. The teachers had always described how the sun travelled across the sky all the way to the ground. They said that no two sunsets are ever the same. Sometimes it just drops into the land and disappears like a bird swallowing a worm, with no trace that it ever existed. Other times it leaves behind a dusting of glorious blends of reds, pinks, yellows, and oranges. Of all the things she was looking forward to seeing, the sunset on the horizon was at the top.

Adnil watched as Star limped around the yard, stopping to chat with everyone in her path, and made her way over to Adnil.

"How did you hurt your leg?" asked Adnil. She imagined Star rolling over in her sleep and falling out of a top bunk during an adventurous dream.

"Oh, dis? My gimp leg is from a fight."

"Oh," said Adnil in surprise. "Why was there fighting in your compound?"

"Let's just say dat I gave dem farmers a challenge and dey did not appreciate it and responded accordingly. I was not dere favourite milker."

"I am sorry to hear that," said Adnil, not sure if she wanted the details.

"Don't be sorry for me," said Star with a grin. "Da condition of da farmer I had da fight with was more bad compared to dis limp. Da new farmers might regret buying me."

Adnil laughed out loud at Star's remark. "Sorry, I did not mean to laugh," she said, covering her mouth with her hands.

"Stop with da sorrys. It's all good. Our future is bright, just like my name. Da bumps along da way just make da walk to freedom more interesting. I know dat somehow we will get out of here and have a better life."

I hope so, thought Adnil. Freedom was so close she could taste it. Yet she was growing nervous, impatient for the day to come.

CHAPTER 20

Adnil dreamt she was free, but woke up disappointed. *How many more times will I have to wake up in this bunk?* Disheartened, she left Sky sleeping in the bunk and went out into the yard.

"I am really eager to launch Operation Thunder," said Robin as Adnil approached. "I hope it happens soon."

"I feel we are almost ready," said Adnil. "We need a couple more practices. Then we just have to wait for a commander to enter, alone, outside of a milking time."

"Time is not on my side. I am older than you," said Robin in an unsteady voice.

"Don't worry, it will happen soon," replied Adnil.

Robin looked up at the sky. "Also, it would be much better for us to escape before the cold weather comes. We are running out of time on that front, too."

Valda charged across the yard straight towards Robin and Adnil, starting to speak before stopping. "Dawn doesn't trust Star."

"Why not?" asked Adnil.

"She thinks Star might be a spy," said Valda.

"Why would Dawn think that?" asked Adnil.

"It's just a feeling she has," said Valda. "She thinks Star's way of speaking is proof that she didn't really live in a human compound."

"What do you think, Valda?" asked Robin.

"Star thinks the sun comes up just to hear her talk. I find her to be annoying, but I wouldn't go as far as saying that I think she is a spy," said Valda.

"It doesn't make sense to me," said Robin. "Why would the Xplerians send a spy into our compound?"

"Maybe they suspect that we are planning the escape," said Adnil.

"Well even so, what would they gain by planting a mole?" said Robin. "We are already locked up. If they suspect we are planning an escape, they just need to increase security."

"Why *does* Star talk differently from us?" asked Adnil, hoping for a logical explanation.

"Language evolves," explained Robin. "Because milkers live in isolated bubbles, each group's language will have evolved within the boundaries of their small world, and thus develop a distinct sound."

"The way we talk isn't distinct," said Adnil.

"Well, you're wrong," said Robin. "Your speech would sound noticeably different from those around you if you were to suddenly move to a new compound."

#

Excited chatter filled the air as the women slowly assembled after the morning milking session. "Snap to it, people," said Valda impatiently, eyeing some chatty stragglers. "Get over here! Chop, Chop! Simone, you're on guard at the door today."

"Pay attention everyone, it's practice time," said Robin.

"Operation Thunder!" yelled Valda, to set the drill in motion.

For the purposes of the drill, Dawn was pretending to be the commander while Aaron and Beth approached her, ready for combat.

"Show me what ya got, milkers," said Dawn tauntingly. The two fighters had no trouble tackling Dawn to the ground and quickly positioning her face down with her hands behind her back. They used long strips cut from a blanket to bind Dawn's hands together.

"That's great, but da Xplerians are taller and stronger," said Star.

"We know that already," said Valda defensively. "We are prepared for that. We have a lot more moves to draw upon if needed. We have been practising for a long time."

"Yeah but have any of ya fought with a real live Xplerian before, like I have?" said Star.

"What are you suggesting?" Valda snapped.

Robin intervened quickly. "We are very well prepared, Star, but if you have any tips for us based on your experience, now is the time to share them."

"Hit da sucker in da knees," said Star.

"Why there?" said Valda.

"The Xplerians are weak in da knees," said Star.

"How do you know that?" asked Dawn.

"Hey, ya asked me for a tip. I give ya a tip." replied Star. "I fight dem before. Trust me, I know."

"Do you have any more tips for us?" asked Robin.

"No," said Star. "Jus dat da Xplerians are weak in da knees."

"Okay, that's helpful, I guess," said Valda. "Remember people, da Xplerians are weak in da knees." This set off a shriek of laughter within the group.

It stopped abruptly, and the expression on Valda's face turned from cocky to stone cold. Adnil followed the path of Valda's gaze: a commander was standing in the doorway!

Adnil silently gasped, staring in disbelief at the unexpected threat. *How long has it been standing there? Why weren't we warned of its entry?*

Adnil held her breath as the commander cast its yellow eyes around the yard. *Is it on to us?*

Tension eased slightly when its eyes landed on today's target, and the patient was led to the medical room.

The yard, which moments ago was filled with jolly laughter, was silent as they processed the seriousness of potentially letting the enemy observe them practising the crux of their escape plan.

"Whose turn was it to stand guard?" yelled Dawn once they heard the door click behind them.

"I'm sorry, it was me," said Simone.

"Simone, why didn't you warn us?" said Valda, glaring at her.

"I'm sorry, I got distracted by all the talk about the Xplerians being weak in da knees and I left my post."

"Well your carelessness almost cost us our frickin' freedom," said Valda. "Come on people, the spotter has to be more diligent. That's the whole point of having one."

"I agree," added Robin. "There is no room for complacency. The whole plan could be for naught if we let down our guard."

The day's practice session was aborted. But by the evening, the tension had receded, and some life returned to the compound. Star brought some stiff new competition to the strength contest, challenging previous champions to defend their titles.

"Wow, that gimp leg sure ain't holding her back," said Sky, watching from the sidelines.

"Yeah. What she lacks in her leg, she makes up for in her upper body," said Adnil.

"Never underestimate someone based on their perceived inability," said Robin.

The women cheered when Star was finally declared the evening's champion. Star's victory heightened their overall confidence and resolve for their impending freedom. The triumphant spirit produced another lively chant.

Weak in da knees, weak in da knees.
We'll knock you down with such great ease.
We warriors will our freedom seize.
We're stronger with Star's expertise.
You'll never stop these escapees,
Cuz you are weak, weak in da knees.

CHAPTER 21

Robin positioned herself in the usual location to begin the education session. Before she could get a word out of her mouth, the door to the compound opened and two commanders entered.

Their large yellow eyes homed in on Robin. Her eyes widened as the commanders approached. They took her by the arms and tried to lead her towards the exit, but Robin's feet stayed fixed to the floor, like a resistant prisoner being led to the gallows. Robin feared this removal was not for a routine medical exam. The colour drained from her face as long alien fingers gripped her arms in another attempt to move her. Her shaky legs cooperated reluctantly as she was pulled towards the exit door.

Halfway across the milking room, she stumbled, landing on the floor. As she stood up and looked back at the women, the deep disappointment in her distraught eyes could not be concealed. Just moments ago, she was ready to review useful information on how to prepare for a new life on the outside. Now they would start that life without her. This was not the destiny she had recently envisioned for herself.

A feeling of déjà vu flashed through Adnil as she vividly remembered the moment when Joy was removed from the compound. Adnil frantically met Valda's eyes. She said nothing, but the plea in her eyes spoke volumes.

This can't be happening again; *not now when we're so close to freedom*! *And we need Robin, the only original left!*

Valda hesitated for a short time, which felt like an eternity to Adnil, then she raised her eyebrows, seeking her opinion.

Adnil nodded.

"*Operation Thunder*!" yelled Valda.

All heads turned towards Valda. This was not at all how they had planned it. There were now *two* commanders to take down.

"OPERATION THUNDER!" shouted Valda a second time, to assure those who were doubtful that they heard it correctly the first time.

The women sprang into action, responding to the signal just as they had rehearsed. Aaron and Beth stepped forward to confront the two tall Xplerians. The second tier of fighters stepped forward as well, knowing all four of them were required right away now that the enemy had doubled. The third tier of fighters moved closer, ready to jump in if needed, and five other women formed a line in front of the exit door to prevent the commanders from leaving if given the opportunity.

While the fighters got into position, Dawn ran to retrieve the blanket full of weaponry. She placed it in the middle of the floor. Adnil felt the adrenaline rush through her body as she grabbed a weapon.

The four warrior-women were positioned in the ready-for-attack stance they had practised so often. With feet shoulder-width apart, knees bent, elbows tucked to their side, hands up, chins down, and fierceness in their eyes, the warriors faced their opponents with intense determination.

The commanders maintained their grip on Robin's arms, but their yellow eyes darted back and forth—between the four warriors and each other—assessing the situation.

Robin had a flash of guilt for being the cause of the sudden change in plans, but quickly put it aside. She lowered her mouth and dug her teeth into one commander's hand, biting as hard as she could. The toughness of the skin surprised her, but there was enough force that the commander yelped at the sudden sting.

The same commander received a swift kick to the right knee from one of the warriors. Its grip on Robin loosened as it diverted its attention to the pain in the knee.

A hard knuckle punch to the face was followed by a kick to the other knee. Bending over in pain, the tall target was in an optimal position to receive an Adnil power punch to the nose with the heel of a warrior's hand.

The second commander was receiving similar treatment. Unfortunately, the bombardment had less effect, and it recovered from the blows more quickly. It took a swing at Aaron's head.

Aaron ducked in the nick of time to avoid contact. The commander continued throwing punches towards her while she darted and dodged, her erratic, unpredictable movement making her a difficult target. But it was the commander who was now on the offence; eventually, one of its swings connected and sent Aaron flying.

Thud! She hit the floor hard, the wind knocked out of her. She lingered on the floor, groaning.

Aaron's warrior partner took over with trepidation. However, she was a fresh fighter, facing an opponent who had just spent an enormous amount of energy air boxing with an erratically moving target. The commander received a fast and furious kick to the right knee, causing it to bend down in pain.

Aaron pushed herself to her feet, mad as an angry hornet and eager for revenge. Her bruised pride increased her determination. Taking advantage of the commander's bent-over position, she dealt a swift Adnil power punch to the nose.

Whack! Stunned, the commander staggered, but did not fall.

Subduing the commanders took longer than they expected, but the women eventually tackled both commanders to the ground. It took all their strength, but two warriors had both commanders pinned in headlocks, while the other fighters held their legs down. Despite this, it was a struggle to get the commanders turned face down with their arms behind their backs.

"I can't hold this yellow-eyed monster much longer," screamed Aaron, trying to maintain the locked grip around its large head.

"I can't hold this one much longer either," echoed the one holding the second Xplerian.

The fighters holding the Xplerians' legs down received some severe kicks as they struggled. Others tried to assist; they didn't have much success, and the turbulent situation was far from under control.

"Use your weapon, Dawn!" yelled Valda dodging a flailing leg.

Dawn smashed both knee caps of one commander with a small hammer, followed by the same treatment for the other one. Several women, including Adnil, stabbed the commanders with scalpels. Xplerian skin was tougher than Adnil expected, and the weapon was not sharp enough to penetrate the unyielding skin.

"I need a sharper tool," yelled Adnil.

A sharp knife was immediately handed to her. The blade of the knife caught a glint of light as Adnil held it high in the air. She thrust it down with full force, aiming for the side of the commander's neck—a fixed target due to the headlock. The tip of the blade penetrated the skin and continued until the whole blade was submerged.

Fuelled by adrenaline and the freedom that was within reach, Adnil ignored the commander's screams. With a tight grip on the handle, she pulled the blade out of the commander's neck and raised it in the air again. Once more Adnil thrust the knife down and again the blade sank into the neck until it was fully buried. Adnil pulled it out again, and this time copious amounts of greenish blood gushed out like a clogged toilet that was overflowing.

This thing is no longer in control of me, thought Adnil as she stared down at the lifeless body in the blue uniform.

She looked over at the other party. Both Xplerians lay motionless, their eyelids covering the sinister yellow eyes.

"Roll the assholes over and tie 'em up," said Valda.

The women tied the large alien hands behind their backs with rope that had been tightly braided from strips of old blankets. The battered bodies lay lifeless in a pool of green blood as the women then paused to catch their breath.

"Okay, the break is over. Time to remove an alien wristband so we can unlock that door," said Valda.

Dawn tried to cut the band off with scissors, but without success.

"Are there sharper tools?" asked Valda.

Dawn handed Valda one tool after another, but none could cut the wristband.

"What da blaze is da wristband made of?" said Star.

"We can use the wristband without removing it from the body," said Robin.

Adnil's muscles burned as she helped drag the limp body to the exit door. The fabric felt foreign in her hands as she grabbed hold of the back of the uniform collar to get a good grip.

"The asshole is heavy," remarked Valda when they finally got the hefty load relocated to the scanner by the door.

"Cut the rope to free the arms," said Valda.

Thud. The long, heavy arms fell to the commander's side. Tugging and yanking, they rolled the heavy, limp body onto its back and extended the long arm up to the scanner—it did not reach.

"Sit it up," suggested Robin.

Adnil and Star awkwardly folded the body at the waist. It took a lot of effort to hold the deadweight in a sitting position. Two others lifted the arm with the wristband towards the scanner. *Click.* The sweet sound of the door unlocking sent chills through Adnil's body. *We are one step closer to entering the outside world!*

Robin entered the medical room first and started emptying any containers she found, rinsing them and refilling them with water. She also looked through all the cupboards for other useful items, including extra blankets. Finding a couple of manual breast pumps, she made sure they were taken along. Occasional use would help relieve the discomfort of engorged breasts as the women transitioned to no longer being milkers.

Valda gave last-minute instructions: "Make sure you have your blanket-backpack and line up single file. If you don't already have a bottle, you can get one from Robin or Dawn on your way through the medical room. Put whatever they hand you in your blanket-backpack so your hands are free."

The group started moving forward and a ripple of excitement spread through the line as those at the front stepped out of their living quarters and into the medical room. Valda tried to open the next door.

Adnil's heart was racing. *I can't believe this is really happening.*

"Darn, it's locked," said Valda. "We will need to use the thing's wristband again." She pointed to the scanner by the door.

Sweat formed on Adnil's brow as she helped drag the commander's body toward the locked door and into position.

"It would have been easier if we had just cut off its hand," said Dawn.

Click.

Shivers of excitement went through Adnil's body as she braced herself to view the outside world. She was mentally prepared to begin the journey away from the compound.

Groans resounded through the group when they saw that the door opened to yet another room. It was the same size room as the medical room but furnished with tables, chairs, and several cabinets. There was another door on the opposite side of the room.

"How many more rooms do we have to go through?" said Simone, voicing what other women were thinking.

"As many as it takes," said Valda. She glared at those beginning to mutter. "Keep your freaking mouths shut unless you have helpful suggestions."

"Valda is right," added Robin. "We must stay focussed."

The women again dragged the dead body across the room. However, this time when they waved the wristband in front of the scanner, nothing happened. They tried again but still no *click*.

"So is this how it ends?" said Dawn with frustration. "We killed two commanders and escaped our quarters, but this is as far as we can get?"

"We are not giving up!" said Valda. "We will break that door down if we have to."

"Yes, we must stay positive and concentrate," said Robin. "There's a saying that when one door closes, another opens."

"Are you sure that's how the saying goes?" said Adnil. "Maybe it's not a door that opens, but a *window*." She pointed to a rectangle situated high on the wall. The light coming through the opaque glass indicated there was daylight on the other side. "That's our exit."

"Brilliant," said Valda.

The escapees created a set of steps. A tall cabinet was moved under the window, then a table, with a chair as the first step. Star scampered up the makeshift staircase despite her injured leg. She tried to open the window, but it was locked solid.

"I need something to smash da window."

Dawn handed Star a small hammer. It took several strikes, but eventually the glass cracked. Star continued until she was able to remove some tiny pieces of glass. Bright streams of light seeped through the openings, like rain from a leaky roof. A small hole appeared, offering the women a glimpse of the outside world.

Adnil could feel the sweat dripping down her back as she watched the scene unfold. She held her breath as the hole grew bigger and bigger.

Star continued smashing until every piece of glass was removed, making it possible for the women to pass through without cutting themselves.

Star climbed back down the staircase and looked up to admire her work. "Here's yer window to da free world."

Dawn was the first to climb up and jump. It was quite a drop outside, but being spry and resilient, it was fairly easy for her. She hollered instructions back to the women. "Try to land feet first and bend your knees as you land so you can absorb the impact."

The physical training sessions had not prepared the women for jumping out of a window. However, Robin had prepared them to be creative and adaptable when unexpected situations arose. One by one, the women climbed up the furniture and passed through the window. A few had to be coaxed through. Two women with large bellies struggled with the dimensions of the opening. Each received assistance and advice on how to twist and manoeuvre their body into a position that would allow her to pass through the opening. The rectangular window was slightly wider than it was tall, so angling the body to give the big belly the benefit of the window's width worked, but it took teamwork to carefully lower them down.

"We got ya," said Adnil, keeping a firm grip around the wrist as they started to lower one down.

"Step on my shoulders," said Aaron, standing below the window.

Her legs flailed around in search of the landing pad. Someone grabbed hold of a foot and guided it towards Aaron's shoulder. Slowly bending her knees, Aaron brought the load closer to the ground and others lent their support, enabling a safe descent.

Simone's belly was exceptionally large—as if the creature was ready for an exit any day—and she struggled for a long time. But no matter how much she twisted and contorted her body, she was just too large and could not pass through the window.

"Go without me," she begged. "Please, I-I don't want to hold you up. I don't want to live knowing that I was the one who prevented everyone from gaining their freedom."

Valda, looking out for the best interest of the group, contemplated the options. "We're leaving." There was firmness in her voice but reluctance in her heart.

"Go, Adnil," said Simone. "Join them now before they take off."

Adnil, the only other woman left in the compound, refused to leave Simone behind. She grabbed a small axe from the wall and began whacking the edges of the window frame. It took a lot of effort, but eventually she was able to pry pieces off, expanding the opening.

"Try it now," Adnil said. "I think you can fit through."

Simone grimaced, reluctant to give it a try.

"Come on, climb up!" coaxed Adnil.

"What if I fall?" said Simone.

"There is freedom waiting for you on the other side," said Adnil. "Take the risk."

Simone hesitated for a moment, then climbed up the makeshift staircase for another attempt. Adnil was right: the sliver of extra space was all that was needed. Aaron was still waiting on the other side and assisted Simone with the descent.

Adnil looked back as she stepped up to follow Simone. Panic rose as she saw the commander move. Soon it was on its hands and knees, moving toward her, yellow eyes fixed on her like a vulture eyeing its prey.

What does it take to kill these aliens?

Adnil turned towards the window. She was stopped short by a firm grip around her ankle. She screamed as she was pulled to the floor, caught off guard by its speed and strength, considering it had just been dead. She brought the axe down hard, connecting with the commander's forearm. The grip around her ankle loosened slightly.

Whack! *Whack*!

Finally, the fingers gripping her ankle fully released. She gave the commander several more whacks to the head and neck until it lay motionless. Adnil watched the eyelids close over its yellow eyes, its bloody body limp and lifeless on the floor.

Keeping her eyes on the commander, Adnil backed up to a sink and ran water over the blade to remove the green blood. Fumbling, she managed to wrap the blade in a small towel and stuff the axe in her backpack.

She scrambled up the makeshift stairway and entered the outside world.

CHAPTER 22

Adnil landed hard, pain lancing up her thigh from her knee. She gasped at the pain. Fortunately, by the time she had adjusted her backpack, the pain had ebbed somewhat. She ran towards a field of tall plants.

She could not see the others, but could see a large machine moving along a wide path towards the compound. *This must be a vehicle,* she thought, remembering the description from an education session. Afraid of being discovered by an Xplerian, she sprinted hard, feeling the wind against her face as she ran for cover. The knee hurt each time she landed on the injured leg, and her heart was beating faster than she thought possible.

After a lifetime of living within walls, Adnil had no experience judging distances, but it felt like she was taking forever to reach the field—and the vehicle was getting closer. She thought she could make out a large-headed figure inside it. Afraid of being spotted, she ran like the wind, her heart thumping rapidly beneath her tunic.

Just before entering the field, she turned to take a quick look at the compound, the dwelling that had been her home for almost as long as she could remember. She was curious to see what it looked like from the outside. She did not have a preconceived image, yet what she saw was far from what she expected. The facade was a rich red colour with crisp white trim. The windowless door was bright blue, darker than the sky on a cloudless summer day, but lighter than a commander's uniform. There were a few small windows, including the one the women had used as an exit. The attractive exterior compound, captured by Adnil's quick glimpse, spoke volumes, yet at the same time, it puzzled her. It gave the impression the operators had great pride in it and took good care of it, in contrast to the interior and its inhabitants. However, there was no time to ruminate.

Adnil entered the field, relieved by the cover provided by plants slightly taller than her. The plant leaves brushed against her arms as she sped along a row, and she was thankful their greenness provided camouflage for the green tunic.

There was still no sign of the group. Many things about the original plan had changed. She could see now why Robin had coached them to be prepared for the unexpected. It was necessary to think fast and adapt to changing circumstances. She was running from danger in a strange new world, but she was alone and running without a plan. A memory of Robin's instructions surfaced. *Am I heading west?*

Adnil was panting. She thought the physical training would have provided the necessary endurance for this kind of run, but now she wished she had worked twice as hard during the training sessions.

She felt far from secure, and an uneasy feeling crept over her that she was not alone. When she turned around to look, she saw nothing. *Perhaps fear is causing paranoia.* However, she kept her ears tuned for evidence.

Swish-swish. The rustling of leaves came from several rows over. Adnil stopped to look, but when she turned, all was quiet. There was no sign of an entity. *Am I imagining it?* she wondered as she resumed running. Again, the leaves rustled, seeming closer. Looking over her shoulder while on the move, a foot caught on a mound of uneven earth.

Outstretched hands partially broke her fall, but she felt the sting as her chin hit the ground. Lying in the dirt Adnil saw the shine of her wristband in the filtered sunlight.

"Darn!" she gasped. Adnil figured a commander had likely tracked her and was now stalking her.

Taking a sharp knife out of the bag, she tried to cut through the wristband. Because of her shaky hands, it was taking longer than she was comfortable with. The sound of the stalker was closing in on her.

Adnil caught a glimpse of nebulous blue through the plants. As the distance between them lessened, Adnil could see it was indeed a commander. There was no hiding from it, and she could not outrun it despite all the physical training she had put herself through. *I'll just have to face it head-on*, she decided. She grasped the knife handle firmly in her hand.

The commander tried to grab hold of Adnil's arm, but she was too squirmy for it to get a good hold. They had learned in practice that a moving target is hard to grasp; like trying to grab hold of a handful of wind. Adnil felt confident that she could stab it if she waited for the right angle. She lunged and stabbed it in the neck, but the knife did not enter deeply. This commander's neck was strangely stiff, and it was even tougher than the skin of the commander in the compound—more like the material that milker shoes were made of.

Continuing to avoid the commander's attempts to grab hold of her, she faked a lunge to its far side; it fell for the bait, which gave her another opportunity. Instead of stabbing the neck again, she used the tip of the knife blade to make a long slit, slicing through the skin.

That seemed to zap some energy from the Xplerian, making it lethargic and droopy like a wilted plant. One Adnil power punch and the commander toppled to the ground.

The commander lay on its back, motionless but not fully dead. Its yellow alien eyes remained open, blinking occasionally, seemingly not focussed on anything, and most importantly not looking at Adnil.

Adnil inspected the wound in the neck. It was dry. There was no blood. *Strange.* She peeled back the skin for a closer look, and exposed circuits with multiple wires of various colours. She noticed that a blue wire and a black wire had been cut through, but a red one and a green one remained fully intact. *The red one must be the primary vessel that provides life*, thought Adnil, recalling an anatomy lesson Robin once gave on the circulatory system. *But wait, Xplerian blood is green.*

Don't overthink it, she told herself, and cut through both wires. The eyes of the commander stopped blinking and stared straight ahead like frozen plums still on the tree as winter swept over the land. Adnil sighed with relief, but thought it best to keep moving in case there were more Xplerians after her.

She tried to put fear aside and focus on removing her wristband. Luckily, it was a different material from the ones the commanders wore, and she was able to cut through it. Taking the band in her hand, she wound up her arm and sent it flying through the air as far away from her as possible.

With the knife back in the bag, Adnil ran, slowing her cadence to a steady pace that could be sustained over a longer time. Settling into the form of a seasoned long-distance runner, her feet performed with athletic precision despite the inadequate milker's shoes. Birds cheered her on, like motivating spectators offering encouragement to a marathon runner. A familiar chorus entered her mind, helping her to maintain the rhythm.

In my dreams, we are free,
Walking together, you and me.
In my dreams, we are free,
Strolling by the deep blue sea.

Yeh, yeh, yeh, we are free.
Yeh, yeh, yeh, we are free.
Nobody is caging me.
Cuz we have found our liberty.

Yeh, yeh, yeh, I am free.
Yeh, yeh, yeh, I am free.
In my dreams I am free
And the commander is serving me.

Well, not that one. Adnil chuckled as she pictured the dry corpse she left behind.

#

Adnil kept running until she was too tired to continue, but being too anxious to stop altogether, she switched to a slow walk.

Eventually, the fatigue caught up with her and she collapsed on the ground. Lying motionless, Adnil gradually relaxed and took in her surroundings.

The earthy scent of the soil and the fragrance emanating from the crops filled her nostrils. Her eyes followed the tall plants upwards towards the sky, recalling what Robin had said about fields of crops grown to make into feed for milkers.

Although she had been hungry for a while, now that she had settled down, she noticed her stomach growling. She put a piece of plant leaf into her mouth. It felt foreign and dry against her tongue. Barely able to chew the tough, fibrous leaf, she spat it out. She found parts protruding, like bottles, from the stalk. She removed a cob and peeled back the layers of green wrapping and strands of white hair to find rows of pale-yellow kernels, like rows of teeth. *This must be corn.* Adnil sank her teeth into the kernels. It tasted familiar—a faint resemblance to the food that came out of the dispenser. After chewing the kernels off one cob of corn, Adnil washed it down with a swig of water and then picked six more cobs to take with her.

It was still light, but the day would soon draw to a close. Adnil hoped she could find the women before darkness set in. *Robin said to travel west,* she reminded herself. She had been watching the path the sun was taking across the sky and once again set off westward. She tried to remain attentive despite her tiredness, but her pace had slowed down to a crawl, needing to focus on each step as she placed one foot in front of the other. If her eyes had not been on the ground, she might have missed the scattering of shiny objects at her feet: milker wristbands.

Feeling elated, she called some of their names in hopes that they were nearby. There was no reply. She was about to call out again when it occurred to her that if there was an Xplerian searching for her, she had just provided a sound beacon guiding the enemy directly to her. Between that and the potential tracking devices scattered on the ground, she was in danger. Adnil took off running.

The cornfield ended abruptly, and Adnil stepped out onto a road. She looked at the tall structures rising up towards the sky on the other side: *Trees*? she wondered, remembering Robin's description. *Yep, those must be trees.*

Looking up and down the road, Adnil saw nothing moving in either direction. Something did catch her eye, however. The road was lined with vines, dotted with speckles of dark purple, standing out against the green. Curious, she walked over to investigate. Thickets as high as her shoulders bore an abundance of dark, plump, little orbs. Long trailing stems sprawled in all directions, clinging to anything in its vicinity. *Are these berries?*

Adnil picked one and put it in her mouth. Her tongue gently touched the sides of the fruit with curiosity as she turned it around in her mouth, feeling the tiny hairs, the curves, and the berry bumps. As her tooth pierced the berry's skin, sweet juice burst out and poured into her mouth. Her taste buds approved immediately. She had never known food packed with so much flavour existed. She attempted to pick another berry and was unexpectedly punctured by a prickly thorn. *Ouch*! She recalled Robin warning of the complex good-bad relationship blackberries had with those that encountered it. Several more barbs grabbed on to her tunic and wouldn't let go. When she tried to remove the trailing stem, another barb lodged in her palm and left a splinter as she pulled away.

Slowly, she untangled herself from the attacking brambles. The lure of the tasty berries tempted her, and the threat of the thorns did not stop her from indulging. This time she was cautious to avoid the thorns and was rewarded with sweet delight without being punctured. Time stood still and concerns vanished as she gorged on the flavourful fruit. When she was fully satisfied, she washed the berries down with a drink of water. *Finding food in the outside world has not been too challenging so far,* thought Adnil, as the blackberry binge triggered feelings of satisfaction enhanced by the release of dopamine.

She resumed walking, leaving the road and stepping over a small ditch to enter the trees. *Is this really a forest? Robin didn't mention anything about trees having a smell.* The warm air and sweet scent of dry tree needles delighted the senses. Robin had portrayed the rainforests as lush, green, and verdant. This forest seemed much drier. Amongst the green trees were many brown and dried-up ones. Teachers had said that things likely would have changed during their time in captivity. That was the way nature worked. Plant and animal species gradually changed over time, adapting to changes in their surroundings.

Adnil's walk slowed as she maneuvered along the uneven, textured forest floor, carefully stepping over the occasional fallen branch. As darkness gradually set in, it became increasingly challenging for her to see her next foot placement, and she did not want to misstep and risk falling again. *In the morning light, I will continue walking west and find the group*, she reassured herself.

Adnil found a level space on the ground, spread out one blanket, then covered herself with another, trying to get comfortable. Her bed amongst the trees had no boundaries, unlike the small bunk she had shared with Sky. The feeling of so much space around her made her anxious. She gazed up through the tree branches at the darkening sky. It was the same sky she had gazed up at as a captive person just the night before. Now she was looking at it through the eyes of a free person.

She had escaped a life of captivity, but she was alone for the first time in her life. She longed to be with the mates with whom she had spent almost her whole life. She also felt she had let Sky down. They had made a pact to support each other, and now they were apart.

Adnil caught a glimpse of the moon through the branches. The familiarity of its silvery glow gave some comfort, and she was thankful to have its companionship to ease the loneliness. Exhausted, she fell asleep.

Fear woke her before she was fully rested. It was still dark, and it took time to fall asleep again. But a bad dream had her back in the compound. The female commander had her pinned on the ground, holding the sharp blade of a knife to her neck.

"Why did you do it, Adnil? Why did you kill the commander?"

Adnil woke with a start and was relieved to see she was not in the compound with a knife to her neck, but instead was lying under a tree, free from immediate threats. She remembered what Joy said about night-dreams: "It's just your restless mind trying to sort things out. Focus on your daydreams, those you can control. Escape your external environment and create an inner world of positive imagery and fantasy. Let your imagination go wild. It's yours to enjoy, and no one can take that away from you."

Comforted by the recollection of Joy's sage advice, Adnil focussed on continuing her quest to reconnect with the group.

The sky was gradually getting lighter, and soon she could be on her way again. She chewed some kernels from the corncob, but noticed there was not much water left in the bottle when she chased them down with a few swigs. Soon she would need to find another source.

Scanning the surroundings, she found some reddish-blue coloured berries on a nearby shrub. The plant was different from the bramble she encountered by the roadside. It had tough, dense, sharply serrated leaves: shiny and dark green on the upper surface, rough and lighter green on the lower surface.

Adnil picked a berry and analyzed it by rolling it between her thumb and forefinger. It was quite different from the blackberry. The spherical fruit was smaller, and the skin was tougher. She placed it in her mouth. Against her tongue, it felt rough and hairy. This fruit was not as juicy as the blackberry she discovered as she bit through the firm skin.

Racking her brain, she guessed that these were either salal berries or blueberries. After consuming several berries and some more corn, she was no longer hungry, but her stomach was churning and felt a bit heavy. Getting used to new foods after digesting the same food every day for her entire life would take some adjustment.

Adnil set off westward. Her knee still hurt a bit with each step, but not as badly as the previous day. To take her mind off the discomfort of her knee and her swollen, tender breasts, she tried to focus on catching up with the group. Adnil could not help thinking how much more exciting it would be to share each new experience with them. She kept up with the solo walk, only stopping when she needed a short rest break or to eat.

When she spotted some wild mushrooms popping up out of the ground, she cut one and held it up for closer inspection. *Should I eat it?* Not able to remember what differentiated poisonous from non-poisonous mushrooms, Adnil decided against eating it. She had come too far for it to end by poisoning. She lifted the bottle up to her lips and tilted her head back, coaxing the last trickle of water into her thirsty mouth.

Her stomach continued to feel heavy and unsettled. She sat still for a while, hoping the feeling would subside. Her mouth filled with saliva. Finally, the food could not stay down any longer. Bracing herself, she vomited up a concoction of half-digested corn, berries, spit, and stomach acid. Although the retching was not pleasant, the expulsion of the stomach contents brought some relief.

After a short rest, she continued walking. When it became too dark to continue, she decided to rest for the night. Lying on her back, looking up at the sky for a second night in the outside world, the familiarity of the moon again brought some comfort, but not as much as she needed at that moment. Her emotions vacillated continuously: overwhelmed with happiness about the escape and her freedom to despondent. She was uneasy in a big, unfamiliar world that she had to navigate alone. Adnil told herself to remain positive, just like Joy would. Despite desperation, hunger, and thirst, exhaustion took over, and she fell asleep. This time she did not wake until the morning sunlight penetrated the tree canopy.

CHAPTER 23

Adnil felt weak despite the good night's sleep. Although her mind wanted her to start walking, her lethargic legs disagreed, and her dry mouth was advocating for a long drink of water before doing anything. Adnil thought of the water fountain in the compound and how she could access it at any time. Now she was free and had never been thirstier.

She chewed some corn and swallowed. The moisture in each kernel provided a bit of lubricant, but not enough. Adnil felt a sharp pain as the food got stuck, struggling to get all the way down without the aid of lubrication. Her stomach felt heavy again, but not as much as the day before, and she was able to keep the food down.

Gazing into the water bottle, Adnil saw all the way to the bottom, just like the evening before. She didn't know why she looked again; she knew it was empty. It was as if her desperate mind was telling her she should doubt the memory and double check to see if it had refilled miraculously overnight.

Still feeling weak, Adnil started walking again. The muscles in her calves were sore, and she had a pain in the back of her head. During the walk, she saw nothing but trees. It was a warm day, and she was thankful for them filtering out the sun. She licked her cracked lips, trying to moisten them, but it just made them more sore. Her throat was dry and sore, and her mouth was parched. She wished it would rain, but knew there weren't enough clouds in the sky.

She distracted herself by considering how to collect water in the bottle if it *did* rain. The opening was not wide and it would take forever to fill. *Could I use the bark of the tree to form a funnel? Will it hold the water or will it seep right through?* Adnil's dehydration was worsening, and she was getting weaker with every step. Her pace slowed as she attentively placed one foot in front of the other, wary of another fall.

Adnil noticed a wide depression in the earth in front of her. In its former glory, this dry creek bed would have contained a stream of life-sustaining, thirst quenching water. Now it was only useful as an obstacle-free walking path. Recognizing this benefit, she stepped down into it and continued placing one foot in front of the other, still travelling west. However, despite the easier footing, she was growing increasingly fatigued. She was not sure how many more steps she had left in her feet.

With determination, Adnil struggled on, continuing until blurred vision forced her to stop. Feeling dizzy, she fell to her knees. A hallucinatory fantasy sadistically teased her by placing a slow drip of water in front of her eyes. *Drip, drip, drip.* She closed her eyes and took in a deep breath. When she opened her eyes, the dripping water was still in her field of vision.

Not wanting to be teased by a deteriorating mind playing tricks on her, she crawled towards it and tried to push the image away with her hand. But the image stayed, taunting her with every drip. The reality of the situation slowly sank in. Her hand felt wet! She put her finger under the slow drip again to validate the revelation and brought a wet finger to her cracked lip.

Fumbling, she located the bottle and removed the lid, then held it below the trickle and waited patiently until enough water had accumulated for a whole mouthful. She gulped it down. The cool liquid flowed down her deprived throat, which still desperately yearned for more. Adnil repeated this action over and over until her thirst abated, then lay flat on the ground as the water travelled to every thirsty cell in her dehydrated body.

After the restorative rest, Adnil sat up and ate a bit of corn, along with some berries she discovered on a nearby salal shrub. After another drink, she filled the bottle and tightened the lid. It seemed to take forever, but even if it took a whole day, it would have been worth the wait.

Adnil continued her journey with more energy and enthusiasm. Since it seemed the creek bed was veering off due west, she resumed walking on the forest floor. Walking at a faster pace now, she hoped she would be reunited with the group soon.

Adnil felt more alive in both body and mind, which made her more aware of the surroundings. The sights, smells, and sounds of this novel environment revealed many exotic sensations. Strangely though, she had heard more birds from the compound, especially when the dawn chorus erupted and woke her with lively music at the start of a new day. In contrast, other than the crackle beneath her feet with each step, it was eerily still in this forest. She walked in silence on the soft forest floor until she heard a sound on the ground behind her. *Crunch.*

Adnil stopped dead in her tracks. Turning around to look, she saw nothing and tried to reassure herself. *Perhaps a small branch or twig fell from a tree, breaking as it landed.* She continued walking.

Again, she heard *Crunch*, more clearly this time.

She stopped, but again saw and heard nothing. *Did I imagine it? Is fear causing my mind to play tricks, or am I being followed?* At this point she wasn't sure which was worse: a mind descending into delusional paranoia, or a predator that had not yet presented itself. She assumed she was still sane, which did not provide relief—considering the alternative.

There was nothing to do but continue walking. Fuelled by unease, she picked up the pace. Again, she heard a crackling sound behind her, louder and closer. The blood froze in her veins. *Is it a wild animal on the prowl or an Xplerian in search of escaped humans*? Either way, she needed a weapon. *Axe or knife?* she debated. She decided on the weapon that felt most comfortable in her hand and reached into the bag for the knife.

This time when she turned around, she saw the creature—only a stone's throw away—behind a tree, with the front and back ends of its body protruding out either side. The large-framed, four-legged animal had short, grey-brown fur on its back and white fur on its underside. The head was small with rounded ears, and its face had white whiskers. It looked thin and emaciated, its ribs protruding. Its long, black-tipped tail, about half of its body length, was up in a circular shape. The creature realized it had been seen and fixed its eyes on Adnil as it modified its posture in a stance with knees bent, ready to leap forward and attack.

Adnil froze with trepidation, deliberating whether to stay still or to run. She felt her heart beating hard under her tunic, but tried to keep composed. She had experience defending herself against Xplerians, but this was a new kind of opponent. She remembered what Robin had said about respecting other animals in the wild. Never compete with them for food because they will always win. Robin had said if you see a black bear, you must walk away slowly in the opposite direction. But this was no bear. Would the strategy be the same? Should she turn away and walk slowly in the opposite direction? The animal did not give Adnil the impression that it was going to leave her alone if she retreated. She was not even competing with it for food, yet it still hissed aggressively. If she turned away, it might attack her from behind.

A lump formed in Adnil's throat. *Am I the food it's looking for?*

The way the creature slowly changed its body position made her nervous. Adnil took the fact that it had yellow eyes, just like the commanders, as a sign that if this creature gave her any grief, it too would face a knife blade to the neck. It hissed at her again. Adnil squeezed the knife firmly in her hand. She readied herself as the creature shifted its weight onto its powerful hind legs. She watched as it wound up and then sprung from the ground toward her. But Adnil, too, had moved into position.

In a flash, the creature was suspended in midair towards its prey. Adnil drew her hand back, then, at the right moment, she thrust the blade forward with full force into its neck, pulling it out just as fast.

The impact of the encounter knocked Adnil backwards to the ground and into a vulnerable position. The wounded creature let out an ear-piercing screech as it rolled over.

Getting back to its feet, the creature turned to Advil—also back on her feet—and stared hard at its adversary, who stood tall, reciprocating the stare. Time stood still. Then, imitating the creature's call, Advil let out a hiss equivalent in ferocity.

The creature took off and disappeared. Adnil turned rapidly in circles, looking in all directions, ready in case it had circled around for a surprise attack. She clutched the knife close to her body as her heart fluttered like a frantic sparrow trapped inside her chest. Her body trembled with both fear and excitement. *What else will I face out here? What's the next challenge?*

Adnil took a deep breath. Her surroundings appeared still—for the moment, allowing her to reflect on what just happened. The walled world she had left behind was cruel, but it was predictable. From what she had experienced thus far, the outside world was ever-changing and unpredictable. So far, she had survived. She had proved she was courageous, valiant enough to take on any challenge. Although exhausting, it was exhilarating to know she had the hardiness to survive.

Yet, at the same time, she wished the worst was over and that things would be calm going forward. With that desire motivating her, she continued on her way, full of hope.

CHAPTER 24

Only a few days had passed since she was last with Sky, but it felt like an eternity. Her heart was as empty as her water bottle had been, and Adnil longed to be reunited. They had shared companionship, moments of melancholy, desires, a bunk, and a dream of spending a better future together. Adnil continued to travel west and was comforted that each step took her closer to the ocean, where she might find the group.

The emotional despondence was superseded by physical discomfort as a blister formed where the skin rubbed against the fabric of the inadequate walking shoe. With each step, further friction only exacerbated the problem. Although the blister served as a distraction from the loneliness, it was a distraction Adnil could do without.

Desperate to find a distraction that was less vexing, Adnil tried to pick out unique patterns—similar to how she had tried to spot shapes in clouds—in the vertical cracks, seams, ridges, and furrows of the bark of each tree she passed. This successfully engaged Adnil's attention until she came across a patch on the forest floor that looked as if it had been trampled down. The ground was scuffed and the verdant ferns, which normally stood erect and taller than Adnil's knees, had been crushed down flat. *Had wild animals used the area for sleeping? Was it a large pack?*

Adnil wondered, imagining them lurking nearby, watching with predatory desire. She could defend herself against one or two wild animals, but was not confident she could take on a whole pack.

As she scanned the forest floor, her eye caught a glimpse of something amongst the flattened foliage—a blanket from the compound. Adnil was drunk with euphoria. *The wild creatures who recently camped here were the other women!* Energized by the affirmation she was moving in the right direction, she picked up the pace, determined to shrink the distance between herself and the group.

Despite the sore foot, Adnil maintained the faster pace for a long time, but thirst and hunger eventually caught up with her. All she had left for food was a half cob of corn. Her stomach rumbled like distant thunder, and she regretted not picking more cobs.

She nibbled the remaining kernels off the cob, then opened the water bottle. It was empty. *How?* She was sure there had been a little water left in it. The bottom of the bag felt wet. *Did I not tighten the lid properly? How could I have been so careless?* Putting her lips to the fabric of the bag, she tried to suck the water into her mouth. The tease of the moisture against her lips just left her wanting more.

Adnil sat with the empty bottle in her hand, anxiously fidgeting with the lid, mindlessly twisting it around with her fretful fingers. The lid spiralled around continuously, never quite gripping to make a seal. Her dazed mind eventually focussed on the faulty lid—making her relieved to know that it was not negligence that caused the precious water to spill. The satisfaction, however, did nothing to alleviate her thirst.

Adnil knew it was pointless to stay put. Her needs would only increase with time, and there was nothing in this area to satiate her. Determined to find food and water, she continued on, forcing one sore foot in front of the other—it was the only choice she had.

Exhausted, Adnil was no longer concerned about the pace at which she was walking. At this point, the goal was simply to keep moving forward. Her eyes scanned the area around her, on the lookout for anything edible. If she came across one, she would even consider eating one of those mushrooms that Robin said may or may not kill her. She racked her brain, trying to recall the difference between a poisonous one and a non-poisonous one.

Adnil could not tell which longing was worse: her hunger or thirst. It was close, but the thirst was the greater tormentor at the moment. *Oh, what I would do to be back in the compound, just for a moment. I would stand in front of the water fountain and take a long, refreshing drink.* Adnil knew she was getting desperate to allow such a thought to creep into her mind. She knew she would choose death over going back to the compound. But it never occurred to her before that one could be faced with a slow death, where you gradually degenerate from thirst and hunger until your body finally gives up and crawls through death's door in despair.

As her body grew more depleted, Adnil's eyes focussed on her feet, coaching them to ignore the pain and to continue performing, lured by the possibility of attaining a delayed reward at the end of the gruelling marathon.

The forest stopped abruptly. In her foggy state, Adnil stepped over a small ditch and onto gravel. Her mind eventually noticed and pulled up the memory of blackberries found along an earlier roadside. Walking along the ditch, she searched, hoping to find some here, but was disappointed to find none. Disheartened, she contemplated whether to walk along the road, thinking it could be more profitable than walking through the forest. Just because there were no blackberries at this particular spot did not mean she wouldn't find them further up the road. As well, she could see that the road curved west, which aligned with her objective.

Adnil's legs appreciated the ease of walking on the flat, obstacle-free road compared to the bumpy forest floor. She had not gone very far, however, when the light buzz of an approaching vehicle could clearly be heard in the quiet surroundings. Adnil bolted back into the cover of the forest. From behind the safety of a tree, she could make out two passengers as the vehicle passed, but could not tell if they were Xplerians or humans. She watched as the vehicle gradually got smaller and disappeared into the distance.

Nervous about the risk of continuing to walk along the road, Adnil went deeper into the safety of the forest before heading west again, maintaining a rhythm of slowly putting one foot in front of the other. She did not know how much further she would be able to walk without food and water. However, the alternative—sitting down to die slowly—was not an option. Despite the discomfort of sore feet, cracked lips, a thick tongue and an empty stomach, she tried to focus on being reunited with the group instead of on the adversity looming over her.

Like an epiphyte plant, she took slow, deep breaths, hoping to magically draw energy and nutrients from the air. The action seemed to help psychologically as she visualized the sustenance entering her body with every breath. The further she walked, the greener the trees seemed to be. The forest was peaceful and tranquil, and in different circumstances, this environment would be a lovely, restorative sanctuary.

Adnil's ears perked up when she thought she heard the faint sound of the wind whispering above, blowing the supple branches at the top of the tall trees. She hoped it wasn't a sign of a summer wind storm approaching, although if it brought rain with it, she would welcome it. The sound grew louder, although she could not feel the effects of the wind on the forest floor. She was grateful for the protective windbreak the trees provided. The noise became more pronounced as she kept walking.

Swoosh, swoosh.

Then she saw it. The source of the sound was not wind after all. In the centre of a dry creek bed was a narrow stream of water. Relief made her spirit swell with gratitude. This stream had significantly more water than the trickle Adnil had encountered previously. Beyond the sparkling surface, the glassy depth spoke to her, inviting her to take a long drink.

She dipped her bottle into the shallow creek, then brought it to her dry lips, tilting her head back to drink. It only partially quenched Adnil's thirst, so she repeated the action. The invigorating liquid travelled throughout her body, resuscitating each thirsty cell.

Adnil took a better look at the beautiful setting. The ribbon of water flowed over a pebbled creek bed and manoeuvred around timeworn stones in its path. Prior to seeing the stream, the only bodies of water she had seen were in the compound. Adnil remembered the occasional puddles of muddy water in the yard. She used to pass time watching raindrops as they landed, each drop losing its individuality as it became part of the collective. And then the big flood. That murky, brown swamp was vile compared to this life-giving water, thought Adnil.

She could see that the narrow stream was flowing at diminished capacity. The hardened, carved edges of the banks revealed the existence of a swollen stream in the past. She imagined the force the water must have had in order to carve out the bank. By themselves they were just drops of water, but when combined, they become something completely different, a powerful entity. Robin had said that water is the most powerful force in nature, that it could be both friend and foe. Adnil agreed, having experienced both versions.

She took another drink from the stream, then took off her shoes and socks before stepping in to feel the cool water swirling around her tired, sore feet. It was the first time being barefoot in the outside world. Although the bottom of her feet were tender, she found the experience to be very soothing. The pebbles tickled her soles while her unfettered toes wiggled around playfully. The new sensation felt wildly natural and liberating.

With her hands, Adnil scooped up water and brought it to her face. It felt refreshing and enlivened her spirit. She took a deep breath and let it out slowly. The sound of the trickling water, the sunlight playing through the tree branches, and the moss on the shaded rocks glistening an emerald green gave Adnil a sense of comfort. The sweet, dry perfume of the forest drifted into her nostrils. *This part of the forest has got to be the most beautiful place in the universe.*

Robin had said that in a forest there is more liveliness underground than above ground. Below the surface trees communicate and support each other. Adnil wondered whether the trees were conversing about the peculiar woman who had appeared amongst them. *If only the trees could communicate with me. They could reveal whether the group had been here, or how much further I need to go before reaching the ocean.* Adnil was intrigued and vowed that in the future she would strive to figure out how to tap into the language of trees. Stepping out of the stream, she put her ear to the ground at the base of a tree to listen. She did not expect to hear anything, but it didn't hurt to try, just in case it was possible.

Robin had said that aside from sharing information, trees were also able to share nutrients via their network. The forest is a community that looks after its members, she would say. How Adnil wished she had someone looking out for her in this time of need.

Out of the corner of her eye, Adnil spotted some blue salal berries she had not seen earlier. Jumping up, she ran with tender feet to the bushes. The first berry was down her throat before she had a chance to bite into it. She did the same with another, then another, then another. Eventually, she slowed down enough to bite into a berry. The mealy fruit was a welcome texture against her deprived tongue. Adnil picked the bushes clean, eating until her hunger diminished. Aside from the physical relief, the distress of thinking she might slowly starve to death before making it to the ocean also subsided.

Exhausted, Adnil spread out the blankets and immediately fell into a much-needed sleep; a sleep too deep for dreams. When she awoke, it was still daylight. The sound of the flowing stream warmed her spirits. She wanted to stay in this perfect place forever, but her head told her she should resume walking. After vacillating back and forth, she decided to spend what was left of the dwindling day at the idyllic spot. The garden sanctuary was her reward for persevering. Forest bathing would be restorative to her body and soul.

CHAPTER 25

Adnil slept well that night, but woke up with a churning stomach. The berries from last evening's feast were wrestling with the water in her belly like they were practising for an escape from a compound. Anxious to see daylight, they presented themselves, leaving Adnil's body from both ends. After the explosive exodus, Adnil lay still to recuperate.

She washed up in the stream, and although she did not feel like eating yet, she felt refreshed and energized. Adnil was mindful of not leaving this spot without taking a greater food supply. She had learned that lesson the hard way. The bushes in the immediate vicinity had been picked clean during her eating frenzy the day before, but further afield, Adnil found bushes loaded with fruit. She took great care to load up and placed many berries in the bottom of the bag. After taking a long drink from the stream, Adnil filled the bottle and put the lid on—and watched it spin. She decided to hold the bottle in her hand.

Although her body tried to coax her to stay in this beautiful spot, her mind pushed her to move on. *Do I put my sore feet back into the shoes, or walk barefoot?* Both options would no doubt result in discomfort, but which one was more bearable: the pain of feet rubbing against the fabric of shoes designed for a sedentary milker or walking barefoot on tender virgin soles. Adnil put the shoes on, stuffing leaves between the blister and the shoe fabric, hoping it would provide a protective cushion.

Since the creek flowed westward, she resumed her journey, walking side by side with her new companion and lifeline.

A faint scent of salt in the air announced the ocean long before Adnil saw it. The closer she got, the more intense the smell became. The soft rumble of moving water became more audible with each step as well. Viewing the ocean for the first time touched the core of Adnil's being. The prolonged suspense and difficult journey towards it made the first sight all the more glorious. Adnil stood still, staring at it, totally awestruck—frozen with wonder at its splendour. *How can a body of water be so immense? How many tiny drops of water are united to make up this mighty ocean?* She watched the waves swoosh up onto the beach, then recede over the pebbles and sand back into the sea. The sound was music to her ears.

The smell of the ocean had a complex rawness to it, like it was not a single scent but a unique combination of many. It was fresh and alive, but not in the same way the forest or stream was. She closed her eyes and concentrated on the feel of the cool ocean air that blew across her skin. Even the pores of her skin appreciated the complexity of the sea breeze, welcoming it like an enchanting guest, but at the same time tightening up, feeling somewhat intimidated and awed by its exotic allure.

Walking to the water's edge, Adnil observed the magnetism of the waves running towards her feet. Leaving socks and shoes on the beach, she waded into the seductive sea, gradually letting the water cover ankles, calves, then knees. The water felt cool and refreshing against her sore feet and tired legs. Bits of the sea splashed up onto her tunic, leaving darkened spots where the water penetrated. She was cautious not to enter further than knee deep, but imagined future experiences where she would fully submerge, letting the glorious water envelop her.

After a joyous time revelling in the water, Adnil retreated and sat on the beach while the breeze and sun's rays slowly dried her legs and feet. Totally captivated, she never wanted to let go of this moment, appreciating every single drop that contributed to the ocean's vastness.

Adnil was amazed at how expansive the sky was from this vista as she watched the sun gradually sink into the sea, illuminating a quivering path stretched across the water towards her. Eventually the sun dropped off the horizon and totally disappeared, reflecting an array of colours on the wispy clouds and sparkling water. The brilliantly lit sky displayed more variations of red, orange, and pink than Adnil could ever have imagined. According to Robin, sunrises and sunsets on the ocean have the capacity to change your life. From what Adnil had seen, she couldn't agree more. If the sun's setting was this impactful, she couldn't wait until she saw the sunrise.

Adnil found a spot high up on the beach where there were no stones and laid a blanket on the sand. She covered herself with another blanket to protect herself from the noticeable chill that appeared with the sun's departure. She felt the sand give a little against the weight of her body as she wiggled to find a comfortable position.

Adnil had no plan for tomorrow, but it did not concern her. She did not know what to expect in the future, but at this moment, she did not care. She was a free person today, and she had experienced more in the past four days than she had in a lifetime. Satisfied and exhausted, she fell asleep.

CHAPTER 26

Adnil's slumber was cut short, interrupted by the sound of voices from further down the beach. The voices were not loud enough for her to pick up much detail. *Were they Xplerian voices—or human?* From such a great distance, it was hard to tell. Adnil's chest tightened as uneasiness swept over her. She walked cautiously along the beach to investigate further. *The darkness of the night will protect me from being noticed. If I sense danger, I can retreat without being spotted.*

As she got closer, Adnil could see a fire's flickering flames dancing against the blackness of the night. She had learned in the education sessions that fire was the result of a fuel such as wood combining with oxygen from the air to produce heat and light, but no scientific explanation could have prepared her for what fire actually looked like. The dancing red flames acted as a guiding light as she continued to walk down the beach. As she got closer, the flames' light illuminated the figures who sat around it.

Her heart jumped as a recognizable melody enveloped her eardrums like a sonic hug. She sped towards it. As she got closer, she could make out the familiar lyrics.

> In my world, I am free,
> Walking together, you and me.

In my world, I am free,
Walking with you by the deep blue sea.

Adnil's mind was racing faster than her feet could keep up and she tripped over a clump of seagrass that had washed up onto the beach during high tide. Stumbling, she fell face-first into the sand. Picking herself back up, she spit out the sand and continued running towards the fire.

In my world, I am free,
And the commander is obeying me.
In my world, I am free,
And the commander is serving me.

The liberating lyrics were followed by spirited cheers that warmed her heart. She was now close enough to pick out recognizable voices amongst the chatter. She tried to call out, "Sky … Robin … Valda!"

However, running, and the sheer excitement of reuniting with the women, had left her breathless. Her voice was weak, camouflaged by the sound of the waves lapping the shore. Adnil thought she could make out Sky's profile as a head turned to gaze into the darkness.

"Sky!" Adnil shouted again. This time her voice connected with the intended target and Sky turned towards the sound. Her wide eyes searched intently until she spotted Adnil, faintly visible under the moonlight. They raced towards each other and collided in an embrace, knocking each other over in their excitement. Rolling over on the ground, they laughed and cried in an enthusiastic reunion, finally settling down to gaze at each other with eyes full of immense relief.

The others, witnessing the commotion, joined them, cheering and giving Adnil what resembled a hero's welcome. Beaming, Adnil stood up and accepted the warm welcome with gratefulness.

"I'm so sorry you were abandoned," said Robin later, as they were standing by the fire.

"Simone told us how you knocked out the window frame and helped her get through. We thought you were right behind us and didn't notice until later that you weren't there. What held you back?"

"One of the commanders woke from the dead and asked for another Adnil power punch," said Adnil, getting into the spirit of the celebration.

"No way!" said Aaron. "What happened next?"

"I still had the axe that I used to knock out the window frame in my hand, so I used it as a weapon," said Adnil.

"And … how effective was the weapon?" asked Robin.

"All I can say is that commander won't be raising its ugly head off the floor ever again," said Adnil as they laughed at the image of it.

It felt so liberating to be having this conversation with the women. Not that long ago, their conversation revolved around the plans of their upcoming escape. Now they were conducting a debrief of the successful escape to freedom.

"How did the fire get started?" asked Adnil, glancing towards the fiery flames.

"Robin knew how to make it," said Sky.

"It took me a while," explained Robin. "I rubbed two pieces of very dry wood together until the friction caused heat. Then I fed it bits of dry moss and dry pine needles."

Robin continued at great length, describing combustion, fuel, oxygen, and heat. Although some women were disinterested in the detailed explanation, they were all thankful for the fire-starting knowledge that Robin possessed and dared not interrupt the mini lesson.

Sky wrapped a blanket around Adnil's shoulders. "You might need this."

It was so comforting to be reunited with the group again. Adnil settled down in front of the fire; its warmth and the blanket protected her from the crisp night air and cool breeze coming off the ocean. Her eyes fixed on the flames as they leapt up from the ground. Unlike some of the women, she found Robin's scientific explanation of fire intriguing and was eager to learn more. *How is it possible that such a magical thing can exist?*

"Are you hungry?" asked Sky.

"Yes, I am."

"We have lots of food," said Sky. "I'll bring you some."

Adnil thought about the salal berries she still had in her bag and secretly hoped Sky had something different to offer—perhaps some blackberries.

Adnil was pleasantly surprised when Sky returned carrying a plate—made from flat pieces of driftwood—for each of them. They were piled with food she did not recognize.

"What is it?" said Adnil.

"This is roasted mushrooms and wild onions topped with bits of seaweed," said Sky.

The rich aroma filled Adnil's nostrils as she took a plate in her hands. She was about to pick up the food with her hand when she noticed Sky using a shell as a utensil. Not familiar with this new way of eating, Adnil was grateful to have Sky's behaviour to mimic. Adnil experienced an orgy of unusual flavours as her tongue absorbed the juices, making her taste buds shriek with delight. Once Adnil finished the first course, Sky brought over another plate with chunks of apple and several different berries.

"I had no idea food was supposed to taste this good," said Adnil.

"We foraged for food all afternoon," said Sky. "I'll never take food for granted again."

"I see you're enjoying the edibles we found," said Valda as she joined them.

"Yes, I am," said Adnil between bites.

"Good thing we have Robin to guide us to the food," said Sky.

"We've been pretty lucky so far," said Robin. "Each day we managed to find enough food for everyone, but that may not always be the case."

"You had better luck than I did," said Adnil.

"Drinking water is our biggest problem," said Valda with a worried frown. "We have to ration what's left in our bottles until we find another source."

"In the compound, we never really questioned where our food and water came from," said Sky. "It was just always given to us."

"But what a price we had to pay to get it," said Robin.

"I am so glad we are no longer in that life-sucking compound," said Valda.

"What a relief that our escape was successful," added Adnil, as she took another bite of the sweet taste of freedom. "All that planning and training paid off."

"Again, sorry for leaving you behind, kid," said Valda. "We felt bad, but we never doubted you would survive."

"I almost got killed … twice," said Adnil. "What made you so sure I would survive?"

"Remember, we all witnessed your superior warrior skills," said Valda, "First you came up with the wicked Adnil power punch during training. Then on escape day, you saved the day by stabbing that yellow-eyed monster into submission."

"What's the plan from here?" Adnil asked, shy to accept the praise. "It's certainly enjoyable to celebrate our freedom, but where do we go from here?"

"We gotta try to reconnect with other humans," said Valda.

"That will be amazing," said Adnil. "But where do we start looking?"

"The plan is to keep our base camp here while we send out a small contingent to explore the surrounding area," said Robin. "If there are others still locked inside compounds in the immediate area, we need to locate and rescue them."

"We also need to keep up our defence," said Valda. "Adnil, it would be helpful if you could resume the physical training with the women."

"I can do that," said Adnil. "We've come this far. The last thing we want is to be overpowered by Xplerians who are roaming around looking for us. Oh, and there's a creek I followed out of the forest. If I can backtrack and find it, that will solve our water supply issue."

Valda and Robin nodded in agreement.

"We certainly don't want to be discovered," said Robin. "I think we should move our base camp into the trees. We're too exposed on the beach."

"Good point," said Valda. "Let's do that at first light."

"By the way, it was good of you to stay behind and help Simone," said Robin.

"Where is Simone anyway?" asked Adnil. "Has the baby come out yet?"

"It did," said Valda, "but it was dead."

"I see," said Adnil, imagining what Simone must have gone through.

"And how is Simone?"

"Not well," said Valda. "She seems half dead herself. Most of the time her eyes are closed and she does not respond."

"It doesn't look good," said Robin. "Simone is very weak. I am concerned that she might not make it."

"What do you mean, might not make it?" asked Adnil.

"Most of the time Simone's eyes are closed, and she rarely responds when we talk to her. We place drops of water and juice from fruit onto her tongue to keep her hydrated. I worry that she might not be with us much longer."

"She is lying over there," said Sky, pointing just off to the side.

Adnil looked and saw a body bundled in blankets lying on the ground. Another person sat beside it, watching over.

"Can I see her?" she asked.

Adnil and Valda walked over to the bundled creature and knelt down at one end so they were face to face with it.

"Simone, I have some good news to share," said Valda. "Adnil finally caught up to us."

Simone's eyes opened, staring straight ahead. Adnil touched Simone's warm forehead, gently stroking it. "Hang in there, Simone," she said softly.

Simone's hollow eyes seemed to focus as they shifted and connected with Adnil's.

"If you got yourself through that window you can get through anything," said Adnil. Adnil thought she detected a weak smile form on her face before Simone's eyes closed again.

Adnil thought of how much convincing it took to get Simone through that window and how valiant Simone had been in climbing her way to freedom. She looked down at Simone's lifeless face. *Is this how it will end? Was that effort all in vain?*

"Hang in there, Simone," whispered Adnil. "You are stronger than you know. You followed the group out that window into the outside world, and now that you are in it, you've got to follow us the rest of the way. You're a dandelion. You can survive whatever life throws at you and come out blooming. We'll do it together."

CHAPTER 27

Joy observed the children's reaction as a large red rubber ball sailed over the wall and landed in the yard. The children watched in amazement as the orb bounced multiple times before finally coming to a stop. *Ahh, new statistics must have revealed that a less bored child develops into a more productive milker. How nice of the commanders to introduce the enriching stimulus object*, Joy thought sarcastically.

The long pause, which hung in the air as the children cautiously examined the strange object from a distance, suddenly gave way to a burst of energy as several girls simultaneously raced towards the ball. Regardless of the reason for its introduction into the yard, Joy was heartened by the pleasure it brought to the children as they endlessly contacted it with various body parts sending it flying across the yard. The novelty of the toy didn't seem to wane as the children constantly craved their time with it. Except for one child. Joy noticed how she timidly moved out of the way each time the ball came near, her face grimacing with apprehension. Joy understood how someone living in an isolated, predictable world might be uneasy with the introduction of a new item.

Other than the ball, stimulation in the compound was limited, but Joy did her best to introduce new things to the children, including mathematics.

"Math is useless," one girl objected. "Why do we have to know about it?"

Joy agreed that mathematics was useless to them if they were going to spend the rest of their lives in a compound, but she hoped that one day they would find freedom in a world they didn't even know existed. Simply being free was not good enough for Joy. She wanted them to be successful.

"You need math so you can count the stars," she said. "How will you be able to count all the stars if you don't have enough numbers?"

One certainly does not need a degree in Astrophysics to look at the stars, mused Joy as she recalled all the physics and mathematics courses she had taken. The years of studying had felt endless, but it was nothing compared to the vast amount of time wasted in captivity after graduation.

Joy believed that, like music, mathematics was a universal language, and that the children deserved to become well versed in that language as well. Joy hadn't always liked mathematics, but she learned to love it. One passionate teacher had helped her realize mathematics wasn't some arbitrary, pointless mental task. It was a language one can use to communicate with the stars. If she was going to follow in her mother's footsteps and study space engineering, she had better learn math. The more she studied mathematics, the more she realized how beautiful and essential it was. It was a language universally understood across cultures, languages, nations, and planets. Sums like two plus two equals four were the same on Earth as on Xpleria or Mars; it is part of nature. Nature grants humans the ability to recognize patterns in the form of arithmetic. Humans then systematically construct more complex mathematical systems that aren't obvious in nature but allow humans to further communicate with nature.

A fancy school was not required to teach the girls about arithmetic, energy, mass, motion, gravity, inertia, acceleration, deceleration, and propulsion. The yard was their science lab. Joy taught them how the world works in a fun and hands-on way. Having the rubber ball certainly helped to explain the laws of motion.

When the children's minds were too fatigued to absorb math and physics and it was no longer fun, Joy would break it up by switching to singing. *Music is a marvel,* she thought, grateful that humans had this language to soothe the soul. Joy recalled from her university days that the existence of music puzzled scientists. Many researchers thought that from an evolutionary perspective, it made no sense that music appeared. Many scholars argued that music was not necessary for survival. But Joy knew otherwise.

To the children, the words could be about anything, but Joy's favourite songs were those with liberating lyrics involving choice and autonomy. Her heart filled with hope for their future as the children belted out the lyrics of the next song.

> Way up high upon a cloud,
> I sit all day and sing aloud.
> Each cloud hosts a different child.
> Providing platforms in the wild.
> Our voices join to form a choir,
> Symphonic notes rising higher.
>
> The sun goes down, we've lost the light.
> I weigh my options in the night.
> Do I stay right here, content to sleep,
> Or seek a new spot and take a leap?
> The cloud is soft, the sleep's inviting,

But bright stars yonder are more enticing.
The heavens call out, with alluring shine.
A bright new star could soon be mine.
Do I stay put here and sleep the night?
Or take a leap, to somewhere bright?

My decision's made, I will venture far.
Today I'll jump upon a star.

CHAPTER 28

Adnil woke at dawn to a day packed with promise. From the new base camp at the forest edge, she could see bits of the bright sky as her eyes followed the trees upward. The sound of the water in the distance soothed her as it gently splashed in rhythmic percussion on the stony shores.

Adnil looked down at Sky sleeping peacefully beside her. She looked calm and untroubled, which gave Adnil a great sense of satisfaction. Adnil wished to always feel like this moment: carefree, with just a dash of uncertainty about the future. Not so much uncertainty as to cause anxiety, but just enough to keep one alert and motivated to stay the course—ready to jump potential hurdles on the exciting road ahead.

Adnil rose gingerly so as not to disturb Sky or any of the others' slumber and stepped out of the cover of the trees onto the beach. The sun broke the horizon like an invitation to a new day, and Adnil's eyes were drawn to the sparkling ocean as it reflected the first light of the day. The water shone like a million pieces of glass reflecting back the light. The rising sun filled the sky with shades of orange, pink, and blue, radiating hope and a new beginning. The salt-tinged air tingled her senses. Adnil felt refreshingly alive and appreciative of the grand gift nature was sharing. She drew in another deep breath and let it out slowly. It was so nice not to be on the run anymore. She had been reunited with the group now for a few days and was feeling rested. Her knee no longer hurt, and she hoped the blister would heal soon. Adnil waded in the ocean every day since her discovery of it. Her body and tunic were clean and smelled of fresh ocean mist.

Two white seagulls began squawking noisily, competing for some edible treasure at the water's edge. Looking back towards the group in the trees, Adnil was surprised the boisterous shrieks didn't cause everyone to wake and leap up in fright. *How quickly people get accustomed to the sounds of their new surroundings*, she thought.

Adnil felt liberated and relaxed. She cherished being able to roam without boundaries, to see without obstruction—a boundless vista that seemed to go on forever. Adnil imagined what it would be like to be in outer space, looking out into the universe and seeing nothing but infinity. She hoped to have the opportunity to do that someday and was sad that it never came to be for Joy.

The sun rose higher as Adnil walked along the beach, trying to stay on the sandy parts and off the stones to protect the bottoms of tender bare feet. Further along the beach, a tall bird stood on a large rock that broke the water's surface. The grand bird emanated stillness and tranquillity as it stood motionless in solitude. Its long stick-like legs supported a greyish-blue body. Its black crown, decorated with fancy head plumes, was held up by a long, curvy, flexible neck. Adnil watched as it craned its head sideways, positioning its eye so it could look through the water in search of food. Its long sharp bill was ready to jab unsuspecting little fish swimming by. When Adnil got too close for comfort, the bird abruptly flew off to a more private rock further along the beach. The birds on the coast were quite different from the ones Adnil used to see from the yard, and she enjoyed discovering the elaborate display of avian beauty the coast was showcasing.

A buzzing sound diverted Adnil's attention upward to an even larger bird. After hovering in the air, the mysterious creature descended with precision to land softly on the beach far ahead of her. Prompted by curiosity, Adnil moved in for a closer look. The nearer she got, the less it looked like a bird.

An opening suddenly appeared in the body of the entity, and two tall figures emerged. Adnil dropped to the ground and gasped, her heart pounding with panic. They headed towards her, and the knot in her stomach tightened when she realized they were likely Xplerians.

Will I be recaptured?

Adnil bit down on her lip, regretting having wandered off alone, out of the cover of the trees. She couldn't get up and run in the opposite direction, as it would only lead the Xplerians towards the group and put everyone at risk. The only option was to let them discover her. Despair poured over her at the thought of being recaptured.

Adnil regretted leaving her knife at the base camp. All she was equipped with was her determination to survive. *Will I be able to defend myself? But wait—the Adnil power punch.* She stood up to get ready for the inevitable confrontation, keeping her worried gaze on the approaching figures.

Hmm, they are not wearing blue uniforms, and their heads are not big. The thought was a bit of relief. They resembled humans but did not look like milkers. One of them waved their hand through the air and called out. Adnil returned the gesture, somewhat relieved at the friendly greeting. However, without a confirmation that the strange humans were allies, she still felt a tinge of uncertainty as they came to a stop a few feet away.

"My name is Adnil," she said timidly.

The strangers introduced themselves as Katherine and Jake. Their warm smiles gave Adnil the assurance she was looking for, and excitement rippled through her. She eyed them with intrigue. They were tall, slender, and vibrant—strong and confident. Unlike Adnil's one size fits all tunic, their garments were fitted and sophisticated, and their open-toed shoes looked comfortable, rugged, and durable. Their clean, short hair was neatly maintained, unlike Adnil's long matted hair.

"We live in Settlement B35." Katherine gestured behind her. "The town was deserted by Xplerians when they returned to their planet, so we took it over."

"The town is growing with new people joining it all the time," added Jake.

"How long have you been free?" Adnil inquired.

"We've been living in the community for almost a full year, but some of the townspeople have been there longer," replied Katherine.

"And before? Were you … milkers?" asked Adnil hesitantly.

"I was a milker until I was set free," said Katherine.

"Set free by whom?" asked Adnil.

"The Xplerians," said Katherine. "Thankfully, just before they left, they unlocked the door to our quarters."

"Amazing!" said Adnil.

"It didn't happen like that at all sites," said Jake.

Adnil nodded. "A newcomer to our compound told us that."

"Many of the sites still in operation have been raided, the Xplerians killed, and the milkers rescued."

"Rescued by whom?" asked Adnil.

"By humans who were already free," responded Katherine.

It was a lot for Adnil to take in. She was excited to learn more about the town, but even more excited to go back and tell the group what she had come across.

"What about you? Are you alone? asked Jake.

"No, I'm with a group who is camped down the beach." Adnil pointed in that direction. "We escaped from our compound several days ago."

"Escaped? Well that's a first," said Jake. "I thought those sites were inescapable."

"Where there's a will, there's a way," replied Adnil.

"We could go meet your group right now but unfortunately our e-craft is only a two-seater," said Jake. "Can we walk?"

"Yes, follow me." Adnil was eager to introduce the new humans to the group.

Adnil was still trying to fill gaps in her knowledge. "So if women were enslaved to produce milk, what were the males used for?" she asked as they walked to the base camp.

"At first the main role was physical labour," said Jake. "Males were used for mining, and for tasks such as building infrastructure, including the milking compounds, and modifying existing dwellings to suit Xplerians. In the early days when Xplerians needed a lot of human-power, most of the males were retained, but once the Xplerians had less need for physical labour, they kept fewer and fewer of the male babies."

The thought of surplus male babies being discarded made Adnil wonder what happened to her own baby. *Was Luna a male who was discarded, or a female saved to become a future milker?* Her mind didn't want to go down that path, so she returned to the present. "Are there many Xplerians who still run milking operations?"

"We believe there are only a few left," replied Jake. "We have been combing nearby areas and when we find one still in operation, we raid it and free the milkers."

"I see," said Adnil as she absorbed the information.

"The Xplerians got rich at our expense, but that day is drawing to a close," said Jake. The mineral resources the Xplerians came to extract are now depleted. That's why they are leaving."

"Once humans are no longer exploited, it will be some other species, on some other planet," said Katherine. "The universe provides enough to satisfy everyone's needs, but not everyone's greed."

"So what is it about human milk that the Xplerians like, anyway?" asked Adnil. "Is it just the taste?"

"It's much more than that," said Jake. "The Xplerians are superstitious and believe human milk contains a powerful ingredient that gives them superior intelligence and makes them prosperous. The younger generation is not as superstitious, so the market for human milk is drying up."

Adnil still had many unanswered questions, but held back for now. She needed to process everything before filling her brain with even more information.

Adnil was relieved to finally get back to the camp and introduce the new humans. As Katherine and Jake joined the group for a meal, they were peppered with questions by an enthusiastic crowd. Excitement mounted as the logistics of relocating to Settlement B35 were discussed.

"We have one person who is very sick and unable to walk," said Valda. Simone's eyes were closed, and she was not responsive when Valda tried to introduce Katherine and Jake. Her breathing was shallow and her skin was flushed.

"She is very ill," said Katherine with a worried look on her face. "She needs urgent medical attention."

"I will call for an emergency pickup," said Jake. "An aircraft will be deployed to pick her up and transport her directly to the medical station."

Adnil listened to the strange conversation Jake had with his wristband.

"Station Bravo-3-5, Station Bravo-3-5, this is White Fox. Over."

"Copy, White Fox, this is Station Bravo-3-5. Over."

"We have a code 4 for pick up. Please acknowledge receipt of my coordinates. Over."

"Wilco, White Fox, coordinates acquired. ETA is 6 minutes. Over."

"Copy. Out."

Sky looked at Adnil inquisitively. "Is that voice coming from the wristband?"

"I guess it is some sort of communication device," said Adnil. "I think I remember Robin mentioning that there were such things in the outside world."

They waited nervously for the medical aircraft to arrive.

"Should we make a marker on the beach so they know our location?" asked Valda.

"That's not necessary," said Jake. "It knows where to find us."

Adnil watched the aircraft approach, flying straight along the beach. When it reached them, it stopped and hung suspended in midair, like a hummingbird hovering in front of a flower. It buzzed softly as it dropped gently to the beach just outside the treed area. A door opened and two uniformed medics carrying a stretcher exited the aircraft and walked directly to where Simone was lying.

One medic waved a hand-held device over Simone's head, which measured and recorded a reading. The other medic prepared and administered an injection into Simone's arm. They then loaded Simone onto a stretcher and lifted her into the aircraft.

"Who will accompany her?" asked one of the medics from the craft's doorway. "If she regains consciousness, it would be better to have someone she recognizes by her side."

"You go, Robin," suggested Valda.

"No," said Robin reluctantly. "I think you should go, Valda."

"No," said Valda timidly. "I-I can't. You go, Robin." Valda stood frozen with fear at the thought of flying and did not move.

"Start moving, Valda! Snap to it!" yelled Aaron from the back of the crowd.

"Chop, chop! Get da blaze mov'in, Valda!" jested Star.

Despite the seriousness of the situation, the group roared with laughter, enjoying the opportunity to give Valda a taste of her own brash remarks. Valda's face, white as snow, conveyed her trepidation. No encouragement could make her go.

"Someone get in here," yelled the medic. "We need to depart now!"

Robin stepped into the vehicle. It seemed like a lifetime since she last boarded an aircraft. She had never flown on one she wasn't familiar with, and this one had an appearance of lacking structural integrity.

Adnil watched with fascination as the aircraft departed in a reverse of its arrival: lifting straight up from the ground in one rapid, yet gentle motion. After remaining stationary for a brief pause, it thrust forward in a straight line parallel to the beach. Adnil watched as it got smaller and smaller in the distance. "Perhaps I should have volunteered to go with Simone," she said to Sky.

"Why didn't you?" said Sky.

"I wasn't thinking fast enough."

"I think you missed an opportunity."

Jake and Katherine summoned their e-craft to the beach just outside the trees. They left with plans to send a team to retrieve the group.

Adnil's dream of starting a new life was coming to fruition. At each step, she had encountered obstacles that could have jeopardized the dream, but had tackled them head on. She was a survivor: wild and free.

CHAPTER 29

Adnil looked out the bus window, watching the blurry landscape pass by them. She felt the vibration of the high-speed vehicle as it buzzed down the road towards their future. Sky sat next to her, white knuckles gripping the seat in front, as the bus travelled at a speed unnatural to humans. The ocean shrank in the distance behind them, and Adnil lamented, fearing she would never see the ocean again.

"Of course you will see the ocean again," said Sky. "Robin said we can do whatever we want in our new life."

Adnil thought about her future in an ever-expanding world. Freedom was still a foreign concept. She had dreamt about it all her life, but freedom seemed a bit scary to her at the moment, almost overwhelming.

The sound of the guide pointing out various scenic features droned in the background as Adnil's mind wandered. Her goal had been to get out of the compound and make her way to the ocean. On the beach, she had celebrated her freedom. She hadn't given much thought about what would unfold beyond reaching the ocean. *What will be expected of me in the new community?* Her focus returned to the bus as the guide set out what awaited them in Settlement B35.

"You will be temporarily housed in the Receiving Centre until new quarters are allocated."

Adnil could see the town in the distance as they approached. Small squares dotting the landscape grew bigger and bigger as they drew near.

"What are all da buildings used for?" asked Star.

"We'll give you a brief tour before we drop you off at your final destination, and I will point out some of the key buildings," said the guide.

Final destination, thought Adnil. She didn't like the sound of that.

Adnil was nervous, not knowing what to expect. The freedom experienced by the ocean had felt intimate and celebratory, but now they were joining a broader, already established community.

The town was a buzz of activity, with people going about their business like ants in a productive colony. Several short square boxes rolled through the cross grid of streets.

"What da blaze are da boxes doing?" asked Star.

"Those are Golems," said the guide. "They are programmed to do several tasks, including making deliveries."

"What else do da Golems do?" said Star.

"Can they make people stop asking annoying questions?" asked Dawn.

Everyone looks so different from each other, thought Adnil as she stared out the bus window. Without uniforms, each human appeared unique to Adnil, unlike the identically dressed milkers. Adnil stared with curiosity at children of varying heights playing in a green space. Some children reciprocated the stare, gawking at the strange newcomers rolling into town.

The guide pointed out the Medical Centre as they drove past it.

"Is this where they took Simone?" asked Adnil.

"Simone? The one who was airlifted? Yes, she is here. She is in good hands and is physically stable now."

A wave of relief washed over Adnil, but she was still worried about Simone. It was one thing to experience a routine extraction when you didn't know or care what a baby was, but Adnil knew it was different once you looked at it and felt like it was a part of you.

The guide continued to point out key landmarks of Settlement B35, including the Aircraft Centre, community gardens, food assembly areas, the Education Centre, the energy station, and the Sartorial Centre—where clothes were made. Adnil was intrigued and somewhat reassured after seeing the results of collaboration, productiveness, and self-sufficiency.

A day bursting with thrilling discoveries finally drew to a close. Adnil lay exhausted on one of the cots set up for them in the auditorium. In the next cot over, Sky was buzzing with energy as she recounted the day's experiences.

"If I am not a milker anymore, what will I be?" asked Sky.

Adnil's heavy eyelids refused to stay open, and her mind was in no mood to discuss future options she had no idea about anyway.

"Adnil, do you still feel like a milker, inside?"

"What do you mean?" mumbled Adnil.

"I mean, does your soul still feel like a milker even though your body no longer is?"

"My soul was never a milker," said Adnil.

The desire to sleep grew stronger, pulling Adnil further and further into a peaceful abyss.

"They said that we will be given private living—"

Adnil was asleep before Sky finished the sentence.

CHAPTER 30

Adnil rose early the next morning and made her way through the streets already busy with people and Golems. The town felt strange, foreign, like she didn't quite belong. She eventually found the Medical Centre and entered the vacant waiting room, which felt open and airy. Wall-mounted digital monitors had unfamiliar symbols crawling across their screens.

A door opened and a health practitioner approached. "Hi, my name is Jayr. How can I help you?"

"I would like to get my feet looked at," said Adnil.

"What seems to be the problem?"

"My feet are in bad shape. I escaped from a milker's compound and have been on the run for several days."

"Enough said." Jayr motioned Adnil to enter the examination room. "Before we start, let's give your feet a soak."

The inside of the examination room—sterile and clean—reminded Adnil of the medical room in the compound, but Jayr's warm welcome and approach made Adnil feel at ease.

Adnil sat in an examination chair and slipped off the tattered milker shoes, then placed her feet in a basin of water. "The water is warm!" she exclaimed with delight.

"Of course," said Jayr. "I wouldn't make you soak your feet in cold water."

"It just never occurred to me that you could warm up water."

"I'm sorry. You are right. How would you know? The longer I spend in the outside world, the more I forget what it was like to live as a milker and not have access to things like warm water—or even know that such things could exist."

"So you were a milker, too?"

"Yes, but it feels like such a long time ago," said Jayr. "So many things have happened since my freedom."

"Did your group break out too?" asked Adnil.

"Break out? No, we were released by the Xplerians. Wait a minute! Did you say your group broke out? How did you manage that?"

"It took a lot of planning," said Adnil modestly.

"If your compound had a high wall like ours did, how did you get over it? I assumed it would be impossible."

"I didn't say we climbed over the wall."

"Well, how did you escape?"

"We had to kill a couple of Xplerians," said Adnil. "I never thought I would kill another being, but our escape took a different direction from the plan and we had to improvise."

"I'm impressed," said Jayr. "I think you are very brave."

"Or foolhardy," said Adnil.

"As you said, sometimes life goes in directions that you never foresaw, and you do things you never imagined you would do. The rescue team would benefit from having an experienced person like you on the team."

"What exactly does this rescue team do?" asked Adnil.

"They scout out locations of still-operational milking compounds and rescue its inhabitants," said Jayr. "Now let me take a look at those feet."

Adnil took her feet out of the warm water and welcomed the pampering as Jayr gently patted her tender feet dry with a soft towel. "You have a blister that is infected. This ointment will help it heal faster." It felt soothing as Jayr applied the ointment. "Take this little tube with you and apply it twice a day: when you wake up and then again before you go to sleep."

With sharp scissors, Jayr cut a hole in Adnil's shoe that matched up with the location of the blister. "This will help ease the pain for now as you walk, but get a new pair of shoes as soon as possible. Throw these things out."

"Don't worry, I plan to," said Adnil.

"Oh, and be sure to come back soon for a general checkup. I want to make sure you are well, both physically and mentally."

"What do you mean, mentally?" said Adnil.

"Everyone is thrilled to have crossed the abyss to freedom, but few find the transition easy," said Jayr. "When you are born in captivity, you don't have the skills to cope in the free world. But you will learn."

"What kind of skills will I need?" asked Adnil.

"With freedom comes choices; you have to make decisions. You will soon be responsible for yourself, and your life will become what you make of it. Also, some milkers need help to get over the trauma of the past," said Jayr. "Some are haunted by painful memories. In the night, their minds are visited by terror, and they only find relief in the morning light."

Life as a milker already seemed like a long time ago to Adnil, with a wall of new memories piled high between their escape day and the present. Yet sometimes in her mind, Adnil was still a milker. The tunic didn't help. She had told Sky that her soul was never a milker, but now she wasn't sure about that. *Can one ever fully shed a label you are born with?* She wanted so badly to have a successful new life, but fear of the unknown occasionally crept into her mind.

"I know it's early days, but what does it feel like to be out?" asked Jayr.

"Um, I was just wondering: does everyone live in a town like this, or do some people live off on their own?" asked Adnil.

"Some people prefer to live a bit more isolated, but in general it is human nature to want to live in a community," said Jayr. "Our brains are programmed for bonding because of the benefits it provides to the collective and, therefore, to the survival of the species."

Adnil thought of the bond she had with Sky and the friendships she had with others like Robin and, previously, Joy. "Don't we choose to be with certain people because we like them?"

"On the surface that is exactly what it feels like, but it is an evolutionary trick," said Jayr. "We need cooperation to survive as a species. Evolution has equipped us with the desire to want and give love: romantic, friendship, and parental. The pull can feel quite strong, but it's involuntary."

Adnil thought of the unexpected pull she had felt when she saw Luna. *Was it an evolutionary trick that prompted me to be concerned about its well-being? If I had watched the other extractions, would I have had the same feeling for them too?* "If it is not our choice, what exactly is making us act that way?" she asked.

"A variety of neurochemicals in our body drive and motivate us," said Jayr.

"What kind of chemicals?" said Adnil.

"It doesn't matter," said Jayr. "Whatever happens, happens."

"Well, it matters to me," said Adnil. "I'd like to find out more."

"A discussion for another day," said Jayr. "One step at a time. What's important today is the condition of your feet."

Adnil nodded. "Can I speak with Simone before I leave?"

Simone was lying in bed, comfortably propped up against pillows, looking at a hand-held screen Jayr had lent her to pass the time. The colour had returned to Simone's face, and she had a healthy glow. She was relieved to learn that the entire group had relocated to town.

"It's a fast-moving world out here," said Adnil. "One moment we were by the ocean celebrating our escape, and the next we're in a town living with other humans."

"Thank you," said Simone.

"For what?" said Adnil.

"For not giving up on me."

"You would have done the same for me."

"Two times I was given a second chance," said Simone. "When you made me go through that window and again when I was airlifted here. I think I'm meant to stick around."

"I think you are too," said Adnil.

"I'm not gonna waste my life, Adnil. I'm gonna do stuff. I'm gonna do stuff that matters."

"I know you will, Simone. I know you will," replied Adnil.

CHAPTER 31

Stepping inside the Sartorial Centre, Adnil was dazzled by the rolls of beautifully coloured fabric. The smell enveloped her, while her eyes soaked in the myriad options, making her want to touch and feel each roll. She was eager to be dressed in something other than a milker uniform and was thrilled that Jake arranged the tour so they could see how clothes were made. Jake introduced Lucian, the tailor, who was dressed in a crisp, long-sleeved white shirt adorned with silver buttons. Lucian came out from behind the counter, revealing dark purple pants which hugged his buttocks and thighs tightly. The pant legs flared out gradually from the knee until they rested on the tops of shiny black shoes, which matched the colour of his dark hair. The women stared in awe at the glamorous outfit.

"Welcome! At the Sartorial Centre, we work closely with each client to bring their hidden person to the surface. Here is an example of my latest work," Lucian said proudly, pointing to a nearby manikin displaying a newly created outfit.

Adnil was intrigued. *Maybe human clothing is just what I need to release the real me.*

Lucian explained the stages involved in the transformation of fabric to a finished outfit; choosing a template design, adding customization, taking measurements, selecting the fabric, cutting the fabric, and, finally, sewing it together.

"The computer does all the work," Lucian said, gesturing to an imaging machine.

"Don't be so modest," said Jake. "Without the customization of the artistic tailor, it would just be a uniform."

Another uniform is the last thing I want, thought Adnil, appreciating Lucian's dedication and enthusiasm for distinctive design.

"I have many types of fabrics to work with," said Lucian, placing a hand on one of several rolls that were standing upright on a large table. "Would you like to see some?"

Without waiting for an answer, he pushed the roll over—*Thud*—and gave it a swift push. It went flying, rolling and unfolding over the length of the table, revealing its full splendour.

"This fabric came in yesterday. It's just divine," Lucian said, brushing his fingertips over the fabric in admiration of the texture.

"I have several blends of fabric that are woven from various fibres. For example, stalk fibres originate from the stalks of plants, and bast fibres originate from the outer cell layers of the plant's stem. Some fabrics include muskin fibre, which is made from the cap of Phellinus elipsoideus, a gigantic, inedible mushroom species."

"Robin, when you taught us about mushrooms, you didn't say anything about wearing them," said Aaron.

As Lucian continued rambling about the minute details of various fibres, some people's eyes glazed over, while others' gazes wandered about the room.

Jake interrupted. "That might be too much detail for people who just arrived in town."

Lucian initially looked disappointed, but relented cheerfully with the invitation to return any time if they wanted to delve into the technical and creative potential of the textile arts.

The group spread out to explore. Looking at the finished outfit on the manikin, Adnil admired how the fabric magically came to life, and envisioned herself in an ultramodern human outfit instead of a milker uniform. "Each of you will be able to discard your tunic and exchange it for a couple of custom-made outfits," said Lucian.

"Right now?" asked Adnil excitedly.

"No, there are too many of you for it to be done right now," said Lucian. "You'll have to come back individually. I am going to be busy for a long time. With the cold weather around the corner, you'll all need jackets soon as well."

Adnil's mind buzzed with the possibilities as she contemplated the fabric options. The colours and patterns saturated her brain. *It will take a while to get used to having so many choices.* She yearned to get rid of the green tunic and its associated memories of enslavement, to exchange it for a tailored custom-made outfit of her choosing. The new outfit would represent her new life: a life of freedom, choice, and individuality.

The women continued to explore, enticed by the visually stunning options. Some discovered a full-length mirror at the far end of the centre—having never seen their own image, they were captivated by their peculiar reflections. They took turns moving in front of it as the stranger looking back at them mimicked their gestures. Not everyone immediately clued in that the stranger in the glass was a mirror image, and observed from the periphery with confusion. Adnil walked over to the mirror to take a look.

She frowned at the stranger that was staring at her and it frowned back.

"Is this what I really look like?" Adnil asked, turning her head towards Sky.

"Ah, beware of the dangers of the looking glass," said Lucian, noticing the expression on Adnil's face. "It should be used wisely: for a brief glance to get the essence of the newly created outfit. But then you must look away. Do not let the curse of the looking glass lure you into a pointless pursuit of self admiration or self-loathing."

Adnil stared at her green tunic in the mirror. *What gives someone in a green tunic fewer rights than someone in a blue jumpsuit? Why should colour, size, and style define you?*

Lucian gathered them all together again. "Each of you will need new footwear."

Adnil looked down at her worn shoes. In the compound, one's shoes had to be falling apart before the commanders issued a replacement pair. Shoes for milkers were designed for a sedentary life, and the recent escape and long journey had taken its toll on everyone's shoes. Adnil was eager to shed the milker shoes and tunic. *How will the new outfit transform me,* she wondered. *Will it change how I feel on the inside?* In some ways she hoped it would, but in other ways she hoped it wouldn't.

Adnil left the Sartorial Centre with a great sense of optimism. As she walked through the streets, she felt a bit more confident than the day before. Passing the aircraft area, she noticed two people looking under the hood of an aircraft. One of them looked like Katherine. She was accompanied by a man with yellow hair.

Everyone in the outside world seems to be busy doing tasks. Adnil recalled Robin's observation that in the outside world food and shelter did not automatically appear; they took work and collaboration from many people. Adnil wondered how she might contribute to this new society. *What are their expectations of me? Does one just volunteer for a role, or is one assigned? Should I ask Katherine about it?* She put away her worry, reminding herself that she had arrived in the town just yesterday, and they likely would not have too many expectations from her just yet. Perhaps it was okay to focus on self-needs for a couple of days.

CHAPTER 32

Adnil stretched her legs out fully, but they still did not reach the end of the bed. The plush, deluxe mattress in their new private quarters was a far cry from the bunks in the compound. Her body felt pampered.

"I'm going to get my hair dealt with," said Sky, towelling off after a shower.

Adnil's priority was different. She could live with her bedraggled hair, but was eager to exchange the milker uniform for a new outfit. She wanted to get to the Sartorial Centre before the lineup of green tunics queued up for transformation by Lucian got too long.

"Are you sure you don't want to come with me?" she asked Sky, not for the first time. "Don't you want to ditch the milker uniform as soon as possible?"

Sky shook her head of matted hair, so Adnil headed off alone. She had guessed right. There was a lineup of green tunics out the door and down the street. She hoped Lucian would have time for her today. She was free as a bird now and wanted her outfit to reflect that.

The wait was long, but worth it. Adnil chose a style that was understated. Lucian said the style she had chosen was simple, yet chic. "It says I feel marvellous, without saying look at me."

Lucian pulled out a chart with a wheel of colours on it. “Now make some colour selections. The key to coordinating an outfit is to master an understanding of the relationships on the colour wheel that look good to the human eye. Harmony versus disorganization.”

“It won’t be green, I can tell you that,” said Adnil. Eventually she landed on blue for the shirt and grey for the pants. Within those two basic colours, there was an incredible array of variation, but Adnil quickly narrowed it down to two choices.

“You have a good eye for colour matching,” said Lucian.

Adnil said nothing. *So much for Lucian’s theory that you need to master an understanding of the relationships on a colour wheel,* she thought. She had chosen what she knew from nature. The pants were a cool grey, similar to the ocean early in the morning before the sun rose. The blue for the shirt was very dark, resembling the colour of a clear night sky during a full moon.

“May I recommend a small colour accent?” asked Lucian. “A tiny bit of brightness will make the midnight blue pop. Maybe making the collar and buttons a different colour? Like … electric violet. That will make a good choice a tad more interesting, without risking garishness.”

Adnil was grateful that Lucian also had time to create new footwear for her. Taking off her worn shoes, she stepped up on the image platform so her feet could be measured. Lucian suggested a pair of open-toed sandals that were open in the spot where the blister was so it could breathe and not be aggravated while healing.

“The shoes can be created while you watch,” said Lucian, pointing to a machine on a table. “We might as well make two pairs while we are at it; the same design but different colours.

Midnight blue for your everyday shoes, and electric violet for special occasions.

Adnil watched with amazement as the machine joined together layer upon layer of material until the shoe's distinctive shape was realized.

Lucian admired the finished product. "The human foot is a masterpiece of engineering, a work of art, and so should be the shoe."

Adnil glanced at her worn milker shoes. They were neither a masterpiece of engineering nor a work of art. They were pieces of fabric barely held together now.

A few minutes later, her outfit was also ready. She walked out of the Sartorial Centre carrying a brown paper bag containing the second pair of shoes and the milker tunic that had covered her body for as long as she could remember. Lucian had suggested the tunic be thrown out along with her shoes, but something inside her wanted to keep it. It was a memento of a bygone day, commemorating the journey to the new life of freedom. On the outside, she was now a transformed person, but inside, she was the same person she had always been.

Except … the dormant seed that had endured a long period of unfavourable conditions had finally been placed in an ideal environment. She could become what she was always meant to be. She felt fantastic and wore the electric violet shoes for this special occasion.

CHAPTER 33

Adnil's mouth watered, the savoury aromas teasing her as she walked into the hall. She looked across the room to the buffet table set with heaping platters of interesting edibles, tempting her to indulge. The communal dinner was being held to celebrate the recent arrival of the new group to Settlement B35, and to facilitate getting acquainted with the townspeople. The room buzzed with lively conversation as Adnil, Robin, and Sky settled down at a table together.

"Is that Valda?" asked Robin, hearing some boisterous commotion from across the room.

"What is she wearing?" added Sky.

Valda was dressed in something similar to the garments Lucian had been wearing in the Sartorial Centre, only her pants were fiery red instead of dark purple, and she wore a black vest, elaborately stitched with gold embroidery, over the white shirt.

"Her outfit certainly is bold," remarked Sky.

"Well, it matches her personality," said Robin as they watched Valda parade through the room, proudly showing off her festive attire.

Adnil turned her attention to the culinary carnival on the buffet table. Her stomach purred as she piled her plate indiscriminately. Her mouth rejoiced as it experienced rich flavours and varying textures. Meals had transformed from basic fodder to feasts with friends. Between bites, the three tablemates excitedly shared their recent individual experiences.

Partway through the meal, Valda passed their table, more cheeky and louder than usual, carrying a beverage glass in her hand. "Thi' party is the best, jus' the best!" she said, slurring her words and grabbing the table for support.

"Are you all right, Valda?" asked Robin.

"Should she be taken to the Medical Centre?" said Sky.

Jayr overheard and turned around. "I warned you not to drink too much of that wine, Valda. You're not accustomed to alcohol."

"I'm cel-cele-brating and making up for los' time," said Valda. "As a slave, I was tol' … where to live, what to wear, what to eat … now I'm in charge."

"I still suggest moderating your drinking," said Jayr.

"Now is not … time to hol' back," said Valda. "I don' wan' *any* regrets going forward."

"Well if you continue drinking wine tonight, you will definitely wake up with regrets tomorrow, trust me," said Jayr.

"No regrets!" replied Valda loudly as she raised a glass in the air.

Jayr rolled her eyes as Valda walked off. "I'll keep an eye on her."

"Why is the drink making her that way?" asked Sky.

"Alcohol is a complex drink," explained Jayr. "It's often drunk at social events, but overindulgence can temporarily mask the filter that moderates one's behaviour. In excess, it can cause problems."

"Seems complicated," said Sky.

"At our farm we used to make dat stuff out of dandelions," said Star, who had joined the table, attracted by the brouhaha. "Dat blazin' stuff could make you forget what planet you're on."

"Moderation is the key," said Jayr. "Self regulation is another new skill that must be learned in order to thrive outside the walls of captivity."

"These are things we never had to think about," said Robin. "Locked up, we had no opportunity to practise choice and self regulation. Over the years, even I forgot."

"And it was dreadfully boring," said Adnil as she finished the last mouthful of food on her plate.

"At the Education Centre they are now offering workshops about transitioning to freedom," said Jayr. "I know I would have benefitted from help in that area when I first got out."

Adnil looked down at the empty plate in front of her. "I am going to get a refill."

"Self regulation applies to food intake as well," said Sky. But the comment landed on deaf ears as Adnil returned to the buffet table.

"Is that you, Adnil? I hardly recognized you," said Katherine as their paths crossed en route to the buffet table. "This is my friend Hamish," she said, introducing the yellow-haired man accompanying her. He looked familiar, but Adnil could not place him.

"Very nice to meet you," said Hamish. "Katherine has told me about you and your valiant escape. We could use someone with your experience on the rescue team. We have a planning meeting tomorrow. It would be great if you could join us."

Adnil considered the invitation. She had been successful at rescuing herself, but did she have what it took to join an organized team in the outside world and rescue others?

"Maybe."

"Ten o'clock at the Education Centre. I really hope you will join us," said Hamish.

This is my first opportunity to get involved, thought Adnil. *Isn't this what I have been waiting for? Besides, I am a skilled warrior, and they need me.*

"Okay, I'll join the meeting, But I'm not sure I remember how to get to the Education Centre."

"Not to worry, we'll send a Golem to come and fetch you," said Hamish.

Adnil finally recalled why Hamish looked familiar. "Was it you two I saw at the Aircraft Centre earlier when I walked by?"

"Yes, we help maintain the aircraft and take them out for test flights," replied Katherine.

Adnil remembered the airplanes she viewed from the compound yard and the curiosity she held as she watched in wonder as the tiny specks moved across the sky. *How lucky Katherine is,* she thought.

"Would you like to get a closer experience with an aircraft?" asked Katherine. "Hamish and I will be flying to another settlement in two weeks for a meeting. We have extra room. Would you like to join us?"

Adnil couldn't believe her ears at the incredible offer. Adnil wasn't sure how many days two weeks was, but she did know she'd be ready. She wouldn't miss this opportunity for anything. There was no denying that she was a bit nervous about being suspended in the sky, but excitement trumped her fears. "Yes, *please!*"

Katherine smiled. "This aircraft is a four-seater. Invite someone to join you if you want. Our meeting will take about half the day. While there, you will be on your own to explore. Will you be able to handle that?"

"Yes … of course. Thank you," replied Adnil, hardly able to contain her excitement.

I will be up in the sky flying. Adnil had to pinch herself to make sure she wasn't dreaming. She had been worried earlier about finding a purpose in the outside world, and already she had two interesting items on her agenda.

She walked back to the table with a plate full of food. *Life keeps getting better and better.*

CHAPTER 34

Adnil followed the Golem guiding her to the Education Centre. *I wish I had access to one while trying to find the ocean.*

"Good morning." Hamish smiled as Adnil entered the meeting room.

Eight others were already assembled. Aside from Hamish and Katherine, Adnil did not recognize anyone. Hamish turned to the group. "Meet the newest member of the rescue team. Adnil has some unique experience combating Xplerians that may be beneficial."

Not sure I have much to contribute, thought Adnil. Embarrassed by Hamish's complimentary introduction, she tried to concentrate as he introduced the others before starting the meeting.

A map appeared on a large screen. It showed which regions the rescue team had already surveyed and which regions remained to be investigated.

"This is our next target," said Hamish as the image zoomed in on a specific zone, showing a compound and its coordinates.

Adnil listened as the group discussed strategies for the mission. *My expertise in gaining control of a compound is from an insider's perspective,* thought Adnil, *but it's a different undertaking when approaching from the outside.*

"Next, we need to bring everyone up to date about what we have recently learned about the Xplerian's strengths and weakness," said Katherine. "To gain an advantage against your enemy, you have to study them." She reminded Adnil of Joy and Robin.

"Xplerians have highly adaptive regenerative capabilities," Katherine continued. "If wounded, their cells become activated and restore the body back to its pre-injured state."

Yeah, I've seen that, thought Adnil, remembering her encounter with a resurrected commander during her escape.

"Xplerians possess enough inbuilt regenerative power to restore them to life even if killed," said Hamish. "However, it is believed that this can only happen once—we're calling it the second chance phenomenon."

Adnil nodded.

"A small number of robot clones are sprinkled throughout the Xplerian population," said Katherine. "These androids are indistinguishable from regular Xplerians. We are not sure if these androids are superior or equal in strength to a natural Xplerian."

"Either way, both are our enemies," said Adnil. "And I can say from experience that both types can be conquered," she said, causing eyes to suddenly look her way.

"We need to know more about their weaknesses," said Katherine. "Knowledge will be our advantage. Do you have anything specific you remember from your encounters?"

"Da Xplerians are weak in da knees," said Adnil.

"Huh?" said Katherine.

"Um … the knees are a vulnerable part of their anatomy." Adnil chuckled inside remembering Star's announcement of this valuable information. It surprised her that a memory of an incident during her dreary life in the compound could now make her smile. "In combat, that's where you want to aim before applying other strikes. It gives you an advantage. And the robots are more effectively taken out by a slice to the neck than a stab."

The room erupted in questions, and Adnil spent the next hour detailing the planning and escape from the milker's compound.

CHAPTER 35

A child looked down at her bowl; the portion size was much smaller than usual. She furrowed her eyebrows. "Why isn't the machine giving us more food? Is it broken?"

Joy looked over at the dispenser. Mechanically it seemed to be working fine, but it was dispensing a combination of mush and air, as if spitting out the last remnants of food in the holding tank. The food, which normally came without fail three times a day, had been reducing in quantity for several days. Some children paid no notice, while others who delighted in consuming their full ration of food were perplexed at suddenly being short changed. Joy suggested to the children that it was a temporary problem, which would likely soon be resolved. However, as each day passed with less food being dispensed, she grew increasingly worried. Joy did what she could to distract the children from the food shortage. "What shall we sing today?"

"I want to sing the song about the unicorns. It's my favourite," said a little one, tugging at Joy's tunic.

"It's my favourite too," said Joy truthfully. "It will be the first song we sing."

After Joy hummed a note to signal what key they should sing in, their young voices joined together like songbirds at sunrise.

A world full of unicorns, a place full of elves,
Where covens of weird wizards cast their magic spells.
Blue skies filled with rainbows, dancing with the sun.
Fairies sprinkling pixie dust down on everyone.

A world full of giant trees, a place full of hugs.
Gardens full of butterflies and orange ladybugs.
A place full of dandelions, meadows full of bees,
Landing on red flowers, swaying in the breeze.

A land full of lollipops and soft chewy sweets.
Small bags filled with candy canes, and all kinds of treats.
A place full of peppermints falling from the sky.
Dropping nicely in my mouth, as I'm passing by.

A world full of belly laughs, a place full of hugs.
Towns filled with loving houses, with fine woven rugs.
A place full of poetry and shelves full of books.
And well-stocked libraries, with small cozy nooks.

A world filled with lots of toys, enough for everyone.
And sounds of children laughing, playing in the sun.
A place full of merriment, a place full of fun.
A world full of wild times and joy for everyone.

The irony of the lyrics was not lost on Joy, and she sometimes wondered if it had been unfair to introduce this song from her childhood, which depicted longing for another world. However, based on the enthusiasm voiced by the children when they sang it, Joy had nothing to worry about. The children were either happy to fantasize about an imaginary land, or they paid no attention to the lyrics. Somehow, Joy thought it was the latter. *There is no way for them to know what a book, a lollipop, a town, or a library is, yet they never asked.* She could teach them any lyrics, and as long as the song had a nice melody and rhythm, they sang the words with gusto. Similarly, as a child, Joy had never questioned the quirky characters or places in Dr. Seuss's books such as *Kwuggerbugs, Yooks & Zooks,* and *Thing One and Thing Two.* "What song would you like to sing next?" she asked.

Knock. Knock. Knock. The unexpected loud banging at the door leading to the medical room caught Joy off guard. Her heart pounded hard as she held her breath. *Maybe someone is here to fix the food dispenser*, she thought. *But why would a commander knock on the door?*

Bang. Bang. Bang.

The children turned towards the unfamiliar banging with puzzled looks on their faces. "What is that noise? Is it thunder?" asked one.

Through the door, Joy could make out the sound of muffled voices. Suddenly, the door burst open. The force caused one of the busted hinges to fly through the air, just missing Joy's head. In the opening, Joy could see a small group of individuals. They appeared to be humans.

Is this actually happening? Are we being released?

The humans waited for Joy to come to the doorway. Joy was speechless as she soaked in the long-awaited view of adult humans. They were dressed in fitted clothing, more similar in style to a commander's jumpsuit than a tunic. Two of them stepped forward. One had yellow hair and was dressed in a brown outfit. Beside him was someone dressed in a dark blue shirt and grey pants.

"Joy!" said the one in blue.

Joy looked at her friend. They locked eyes for a moment, then wrapped their arms around each other, bodies clinging in a warm embrace. Time stood still, giving them a moment to absorb what had just happened. Joy was the first to let go. She stepped back, holding Adnil at arm's length.

"I thought I would never see you again," said Adnil through tears. "When they took you away, I-I thought that was … the end."

Joy looked at Adnil with compassion. "I'm so sorry for what you must have gone through, not knowing. In the end, my new life wasn't so bad. They gave me a new role, caring for children. What about you Adnil, did you get released?"

"No, we broke out of the compound ourselves, but I got separated from the group. I travelled all the way to the ocean alone and reconnected with the group there."

"That's amazing," said Joy. "So, you didn't run into any problems?"

"Well, I didn't say that," said Adnil. "I ran into many problems, but I will save those stories for another time."

Adnil introduced Hamish, who greeted Joy with a generous smile and eyes that were sincere. "It's a pleasure to meet you, Joy."

His smile warmed her like the appearance of the sun on a cloudy day. It had been a long time since she'd seen anybody other than the children.

"The Xplerians who held you in captivity are no longer here," said Hamish. "It appears, from what we have seen so far, that they left a few days ago."

"That might explain why the dispenser is running low on food," said Joy as she put the pieces together.

"Things are changing in the outside world," said Hamish. "Many of the Xplerians have returned to their home planet."

"What's going on?" One of the older girls approached Joy at the doorway.

"Everything is fine," said Joy. "These people are here to help us. Go back and sit with the other children. I will come and explain in a moment." She turned back to Hamish. "I thought I might find freedom in my lifetime, but it was starting to feel like it would never happen. Where will we go when we leave this place?"

"We will take you to the town where I live now," said Adnil. "Settlement B35. You will love it, Joy, and everyone will be so excited to see you."

"Give me a moment with the children," said Joy. "I need to prepare them for their first step into a world they don't know exists."

Joy gathered the children around her. She was thankful she had encouraged the girls to use their imaginations. Since they were already accustomed to dreaming up make-believe lands and characters, the story she was about to tell them would not be beyond them.

"We are about to go on an exciting journey, children, except this one will be a real journey, not an imaginary one. There is another world just through that open door," Joy began. "Imagine a world with a very big yard. It is so big that you cannot see the walls because they are too far away from your eyes. Just think how much room you will have to run and play! There are other humans in the world too, not just us. These kind people who came to our door will help us get to a nicer home in that world. Isn't this exciting?"

"Will we still be able to have story time in that world?" asked a child.

"Yes," replied Joy, smiling.

“What about singing sessions?” asked another.

“Yes, there will be singing as well,” said Joy.

“Where will we sleep? Will we sleep on clouds like Skookum did?” asked one of the younger children, not yet able to differentiate between the real world Joy was trying to present and an imaginary one.

“Skookum is not real,” said a child a little bit older—rolling her eyes with a look of impatience and intellectual superiority.

“We will have very cozy beds,” assured Joy. “But I can’t tell you everything, or it will leave no room for surprises.”

“I don’t want to go. I’m scared.” One child began to cry.

“Going to a new place and starting a new life can be scary,” said Joy. “But not everything will be strange. We have each other. That won’t change. The sky, the clouds, and the sun will look the same out there as they do from the yard, maybe even better.”

“We don’t have a choice anyway. We can’t stay here with a broken food dispenser,” came a voice of reason from one of the older children.

The reassurance that the children weren’t going to starve to death was an immense relief for Joy. She wouldn’t have been able to bear witnessing it.

“We have to walk for a while before we get to our new home,” said Joy. “It might not actually be very far, but it will seem like a long walk because we are not used to a big world.”

When Joy finished, she asked Hamish and Adnil to come inside so the children would know who they were travelling with. Joy and Adnil stood arm in arm, watching the curiosity in the children’s eyes as Hamish spoke. The children were taken with him immediately as he used his reassuring voice and soulful eyes to paint a picture of an exciting journey to a magical world full of adventures and opportunities.

"The world is very spacious, so it is important to stay close to each other," Joy reminded the children as they gathered by the exit door.

The wide-open space took her breath away as Joy once again stepped into the outside world. But it felt different this time. This step was permanent and was done amongst friends. It was a long time coming.

In single file, the children followed Hamish through the medical room and out of the confines of the compound into the free world. Like a bird coaxing its fledglings to leave the nest and take their first flight, Joy stood at the door and encouraged them to trust their wings. She watched proudly as each child carefully took their first step, looking around in wonder at the vast surroundings. Joy felt a weight lift off her shoulders. She had agonized during her role as caregiver, hoping for a swift release so as few as possible would have to experience the traumatic life of a milker. Now they were liberated, ready to face a new chapter in their life with curiosity and renewed energy. The possibilities for their future were endless.

CHAPTER 36

"Another chair?" Adnil asked as Sky dragged the piece of furniture through the door.

"Valda didn't want it in her quarters, so I said I would take it," said Sky.

"With our chairs, plus the chair Star gave you, and now this one from Valda … it's getting a bit crowded in here."

"There's lots of space," said Sky, as she started rearranging the furniture.

"Well, please don't move any more stuff in here," Adnil snapped.

"Relax, Adnil."

Adnil watched Sky squeeze the chair into a corner. "Why are you still wearing that milker uniform, Sky? Don't you want to get a new outfit?"

"I haven't got around to it yet."

"Well I hope you do it soon. I don't understand why you haven't done it already." Adnil stormed out the door.

Thank goodness for walking. Adnil hoped a long walk would clear her mind of the disagreement. During her escape, walking was a mode of transportation: fleeing from danger towards a new beginning. Today Adnil walked with no particular destination in mind, just curiously exploring streets and pathways to see where they would take her. The buildings thinned as she ventured towards the outskirts of the settlement. Eventually, there were no buildings at all, just a roadway that led to who knows where.

Curious, she followed it for a short distance, but stopped suddenly as a tinge of fear sent shivers of doubt through her mind. The familiar quarters she and Sky now called home suddenly felt so far away. Adnil reached in her pocket to feel the fob she could use to summon a Golem if she got lost. *Have I been reckless to assume the technology would work regardless of how far I venture from the settlement?* She fought a rising panic, as she regretted allowing the device in her pocket to give her false reassurance. *As a warrior in the forest, I relied on my own instincts and survived. Why am I now relying on a toy in my pocket?*

Adnil was about to turn back when she saw two beings approaching. Her heart thumped faster, just like it did the day she saw the two figures on the beach. Her feet froze in place. And just like that day on the beach, she wondered if it had been a mistake to venture off so far alone again. *Will I always have this haunting feeling,* she wondered as her hand gripped the fob in her pocket.

As the distance between her and the two figures diminished, Adnil could see a couple holding hands as they walked. One of them had distinct yellow hair.

"Adnil, is that you?" shouted Joy.

Relief washed over Adnil at the sound of her friend's voice.

"Where are you off to, Adnil?" asked Joy when they got closer.

"Nowhere in particular, just exploring," Adnil replied.

"I'll leave you two to catch up," said Hamish. "I've got to review some plans before tomorrow's meeting. See you later,"— he gently kissed Joy on the forehead—"and see you tomorrow, Adnil."

"Isn't it grand out here?" said Joy, looking up at the vast sky with a sparkle in her eye.

"Remember all the times we spent together in the yard looking up at the sky, dreaming of freedom," said Adnil. "And here we are, in the outside world, and what are we doing?"

"Looking up at the sky!" they said in unison.

"Yeah, and it's the same sky. That part has not changed," said Joy.

"What are your plans now?" asked Adnil, as they turned back towards the town. "Will you get back into space engineering?"

"Pre-colonization I had signed up for a space mission—I was actually waiting to hear if I had been accepted. I still have a strong desire to explore the unknown and to discover new worlds … in fact, even more now."

"I have no doubt they would accept you," said Adnil.

"But it's such a long time since I lived on the outside. I can't just continue where I left off," said Joy. "Maybe the Education Centre will help me brush up on my knowledge. Maybe the world wide web will help."

"The what?" asked Adnil.

"I've been in the outside world before, but for you, it is brand new." A look of concern passed over Joy's features. "How are you coping, Adnil?"

"Well, our quarters are nice. My new outfit is wonderful, and the community is so helpful," said Adnil with a long face.

"What's wrong, Adnil?"

"Sky has changed since we moved to the settlement."

"And?"

"And what?"

"Isn't it good that she's changing now that she's in the outside world?"

"But we don't think the same way anymore," said Adnil. "I can't understand why she is still wearing that milker uniform now that we are finally free."

"To you it's a symbol of enslavement, but maybe to Sky, it is just a piece of clothing."

"Yeah, but ... still," responded Adnil. "A milker uniform?"

"In a way, a relationship in captivity is easier," said Joy. "Everything is predictable: no choices or surprises. Now your world has opened up; you are on a new journey together. There are no walls dictating boundaries, so you have to set your own boundaries."

"I had no idea relationships would be more difficult on the outside."

"Welcome to the real world," said Joy. "You will both have to go through an adjustment period, where you and Sky learn to live together, yet apart. It's important for each of you to grow as independent, unique individuals. Your lives will still intersect and over time you will determine where you are both comfortable having them intersect."

"In the compound we made a promise we'd always support each other," said Adnil.

"Having a partner isn't about having someone to carry the weight of the world for you," said Joy. "It's about having someone whose journey complements your own. Let go of your expectations during this adjustment period. Unrealistic expectations can be a relationship killer. When expectations don't align, it makes you miserable, and it alienates your partner."

"Maybe Sky and I should go separate ways," said Adnil.

"If that's what you really want," replied Joy.

Adnil shrugged, thinking maybe she could compromise about the chairs, but living with someone still wearing a milker uniform was asking a lot.

"Focus on opportunities for yourself," said Joy. "Look at what you have accomplished so far, Adnil. You were part of the rescue team that gave me my freedom. And Hamish tells me you and Sky will be joining them on the flight tomorrow. That's exciting!"

"I am looking forward to it." Adnil smiled. "From the yard I would watch the aircraft, trying to figure out how it could stay suspended up there. I never dreamt I would be inside one of them one day, flying across the sky."

"It's time to make your dreams happen," said Joy. "I was hoping this day would come for you, Adnil. I have a question written in pre-colonization days by a poet named Oliver. At times I thought it would forever remain an anachronism."

"What question is that?" said Adnil.

"Tell me, what is it you plan to do with your one wild and precious life?"

Silence hung in the air as Adnil thought about the question. Adnil envied Joy. Joy had a goal. Adnil wasn't sure what to do with her precious life now that she was free.

At least I have a plan for tomorrow.

"Maybe I'll be a pilot one day," she said with a grin.

CHAPTER 37

Despite having trouble sleeping due to the excitement of their upcoming flight, both Adnil and Sky were out of bed and at the Aircraft Centre to meet Katherine and Hamish just after sunrise.

Adnil was dressed in her new garb. Sky was still wearing the green tunic, but with new shoes and proudly sporting a fresh look of short red curls.

Katherine and Hamish climbed into the front seats aboard the aircraft, and Adnil and Sky positioned themselves in the two seats behind. Adnil watched with intrigue as Katherine programmed the computer screen on the dashboard.

"This aircraft has a gimballed propulsion system," said Hamish, turning to explain to the passengers. "It can provide thrust in any direction without need for rudders or tailplane control."

Adnil and Sky listened with awe, not fully comprehending but still interested.

"The advantage of this system is that these planes are quiet and ride gently and smoothly," said Katherine.

The aircraft lifted off the ground, shooting straight up into the air quickly and quietly. The buildings in the town shrank as they rose high above it. Adnil felt like her stomach was left behind on the ground. Her eyes were glued to the window. For a moment the aircraft remained motionless, suspended in the sky directly above the town, like a bee hovering over a flower. Then it advanced forward at high speed.

As she gazed ahead into the vast sky, Adnil saw the aircraft's shadow on a cloud. The image looked like it was surrounded by a multi-colour circle, like the halo she had sometimes seen around the sun or moon.

"What is that rainbow circle?" asked Sky when she spotted it.

"It is an optical phenomenon known as the glory," said Katherine. "You need the sun to be directly behind your head and a cloud in front. The aircraft's shadow shows up on the cloud. When it is surrounded by a multi-coloured circle of light, that's the glory. The plane's shadow doesn't have anything to do with making the glory. But when the glory and the shadow just happen to be located in the same direction, it's kinda cool to view."

The plane picked up speed, and Adnil felt an incredible rush as they blasted through the air. Looking out the window gave her a bird's-eye view of the region and evoked a feeling of power and freedom as they soared over the land.

Hamish talked at great length about the upcoming meeting, mentioning things such as determining how many Xplerians were left on Earth and their locations, the estimated number of humans still in bondage, and how to free them. "How will the fragmented pieces of human civilization be sewn back together?"

"It would be good to know whether all the current human settlements are self-sufficient," said Katherine. "If not, how can we close the gaps? Self-sufficiency is the key to survival."

"That's for sure," said Hamish. "The history books make that apparent. Your trading partners are your friends … until they don't need you anymore."

Any other time Adnil would have found this discussion fascinating, but at the moment she was only half listening and absorbed with the miracle of flying. The marvel of sitting still in a chair, but at the same time travelling through the air at a rapid pace, astounded her. She wished she could enjoy her special moment without background chatter.

"They say that communication has been re-established with the colony of humans on Mars," continued Hamish.

"A silver lining of the Xplerians taking control of the planet was that it unified the nations on Earth," said Katherine. "It was the great equalizer. The national borders have dissolved. Internal disputes vanished as we became united against our common enemy."

"What a price we had to pay to finally reach global peace and unity," said Hamish.

Finally, there was a long pause in the conversation and Adnil focussed all her attention on the wonder of being suspended in the air. Looking inland, she could see mountain peaks popping their pointy heads up over bands of clouds. She glanced over to look through Sky's window and could see the ocean in the distance. Small whitecap waves appeared to be stationary against a static sea. The dark blue sea contained patches of lighter greenish-blue sections, making Adnil curious to know what caused the colour irregularity.

Sky was less enthusiastic about looking out the window. Her hands gripped the seat in front of her, and other than occasional glances out the window, she kept her gaze forward.

"Would you like to fly the plane on the way back?" said Katherine.

"Me?" said Adnil in surprise.

"Well, actually the plane practically flies itself, but once we are up in the air and level, we can switch it from automatic to manual, so you get the feel of operating an aircraft."

"Isn't that dangerous?" asked Sky, nervously.

"There's an override built in," said Hamish. "If it looks like Adnil is about to crash the aircraft, it will intervene."

#

They started their descent. Adnil could see random orange dots of deciduous trees starting to change colour at the cusp of the autumn season. Buildings that looked like tiny rectangles got bigger and bigger the closer they got to the ground. Eventually, the aircraft made a soft landing on its target. All four passengers climbed out as soon as the doors opened.

Sky sat on the ground to recuperate from the unsettling effects of the flight as they were welcomed by Trenton, a town representative. "We have contingents from twenty-two settlements joining us for the meeting," said Trenton. "In addition, representatives from the Mars colony will be joining via tele-chat."

Sky got to her feet to survey the surroundings, observing the townspeople milling about. She let out a piercing scream and ran back to the aircraft and frantically climbed on board. "Everyone get in, get in! We need to leave now!"

Adnil had never seen such terror in Sky's eyes before. "What's the matter, Sky?"

"I-I saw one!" said Sky. "Come on, let's go." She pulled on Adnil's arm.

"What did you see, Sky?" asked Hamish.

"An Xplerian! Quick, Adnil. Get in! We have to get out of here before we're recaptured."

Adnil looked in the direction Sky had been looking and her eyes widened. *There it is!* Although it was not wearing a blue jumpsuit, it was certainly an Xplerian—even from a distance, there was no mistaking the large Xplerian head and tall body. Adnil's hands shook. She regretted not bringing her knife. She hadn't thought it would be required on this trip.

"Hurry up! Get in!" cried Sky.

"It's all right," said Trenton. "They are harmless. You have nothing to worry about."

"What do you mean, Trenton?" said Hamish. "Why is it here?"

"We have two Xplerians living amongst us," said Trenton. "They deserted the Xplerian community ages ago and joined ours. They live harmoniously with humans in this community. I'm sorry, I should have alerted you."

"Can they be trusted?" said Hamish.

"How can you be sure they are not just infiltrating the community?" said Katherine.

"They can be trusted," said Trenton. "They have been with us quite a while and have contributed much. Their knowledge has been instrumental in us freeing many humans."

"And people accept the fact that Xplerians live amongst them?" asked Katherine.

"It took some people a while to get used to the idea," said Trenton. "But now it is fine. They have been living with us for so long I forget that not long ago it would have been unheard of."

Katherine cocked her head towards Adnil and Sky. "These two were still enslaved as milkers less than three weeks ago. I wouldn't have suggested they accompany us if I had known."

Trenton looked chagrined and turned to Sky. "I am very sorry that my forgetfulness resulted in such an unpleasant start to your visit."

Although the thought of having Xplerians as allies with humans seemed impossible to Adnil, she decided to trust Trenton. *The outside world is full of surprises, and there is so much more to learn.*

Once Sky had calmed, Katherine, Hamish, and Trenton left to attend the meeting, and she and Adnil walked around the town. It was similar to their newly adopted town, if not a bit smaller. Sky's tunic made it apparent that they were recent arrivals to the free world, and they received extra-welcoming smiles, and noticed kind acknowledgement in the eyes of people they passed.

"What if we run into one of the Xplerians?" said Sky.

"I guess we have to trust that it is all right," said Adnil.

"There's one." Sky squeezed Adnil's hand tighter. "There's an Xplerian."

Adnil subconsciously stepped in front of Sky, trying to block the sight of her milker uniform. They observed from a distance as it worked side by side with humans, loading boxes onto a platform.

"It's not wearing a commander uniform, but it is definitely an Xplerian," said Adnil.

The Xplerian came to the aid of a human struggling to lift an extra-large box.

“It seems considerate and helpful,” said Sky.

“People are capable of change,” said Adnil.

“Yeah, but it is not a person.”

“I guess it doesn’t matter what species it is,” said Adnil. “It’s not human, but it is still a being and capable of change.”

“Yes, I guess you’re right.”

“Besides, it wouldn’t be fair to hold it accountable for the bad actions of an entire group.”

“So if every being is capable of change, is it possible for change to happen in the other direction?” asked Sky.

“What do you mean, the other direction?”

“I mean, if you are a good being, can you change and become a monster?”

“I guess it’s possible. Joy said that everyone has the potential to do both good and evil.”

“I wonder what causes one to be a good person or a bad person,” said Sky.

“I don’t think you are ever totally one or the other,” said Adnil thoughtfully. “I think even good people experience times when badness pops up, which they justify when the bad action benefits them. Sometimes people are too lazy or self-centred to be good all the time.”

As they turned a corner, Adnil and Sky spotted a group of toddlers in yellow uniforms, gathered in a green space. Two women were with them, both in milker uniforms.

“Do you think these are new arrivals to this town?” asked Sky, staring.

A short while ago it was them who had just arrived in a settlement. Now they were the veterans witnessing another group of new arrivals.

Adnil watched the adults struggle to keep the children together. The youngest ones chirped incessantly, like a clutch of baby birds calling for attention, while bigger ones were crawling, or walking on new found legs towards nearby streets. Adnil envied these children who would have no other memory but freedom. The overwhelmed adults tried to keep the little ones contained, but in a world without walls, it was an impossible task. *Maybe we can assist. After all, everyone has been so helpful to us.*

Sky was one step ahead of her. "Oh no you don't, little one," she said as she scooped up a toddler on its hands and knees making a beeline towards the street.

The shriek of one particular toddler triggered a familiar emotion in Adnil. She felt curiously drawn to the energetic little creature, who was crawling rapidly and heading straight for the roadway. Adnil raced over and plucked it out of the path of a passing Golem. The child turned its face towards the intervening guardian. Familiar brown eyes connected with Adnil's—eyes of the same colour—but there was something more striking: a crescent moon birthmark! Adnil's mind overflowed with emotion, like a river joining a waterfall after a long journey.

The baby looked different from that day in the medical room. It was bigger, stronger, and heftier, but there was no mistaking that this was her baby. Adnil felt the softness of the child's face against her cheek as she held it tight. Its hair, which hadn't had time to become matted in its short life, smelled of fresh rainwater.

"This is my baby," Adnil said to Sky. "Its name is Luna."

CHAPTER 38

Adnil watched the town dwindle as the aircraft ascended, the buildings appearing smaller by the second. She sat with Katherine in the front seats.

From the back, Hamish was filling them in about the meeting. "There was an Xplerian present who provided information about the locations of the milker compounds. They also revealed valuable facts about the Xplerians that will be beneficial when we strategize about retaking the remaining compounds."

"Yes, it's useful to have a one or two on our side," said Katherine.

"Such an interesting species," said Hamish. "Their eyes are quite different from ours."

"Well, that's not hard to miss," said Sky. "Those big yellow eyes are pretty much the first thing you see."

"I don't just mean the size and colour," said Hamish. "Did you know they can see a whole range of colours that we can't see?"

"Just like birds," said Katherine.

"What do you mean, just like birds?" said Adnil.

"Birds have vision that can discern colours in the ultraviolet range, beyond the rainbow that we see. Many bird species possess a fourth type of colour receptor," said Katherine.

"Did you know they are androgenous?" said Hamish.

"Birds?" asked Sky.

"No, I mean Xplerians," said Hamish. "If they want to procreate, they temporarily choose a gender. After they mate and produce offspring, they revert back to being androgenous."

"That's brilliant," said Katherine.

"So Valda was right," said Adnil, remembering debating the sex of the commanders. That day seemed like such a long time ago. In contrast, now they were flying home from a meeting where humans and Xplerians sat around the same table. Adnil thought about bird vision. There was so much to learn, and she looked forward to a lifetime of discovering new knowledge.

"Do you want to take manual control of the aircraft now?" asked Katherine once they were cruising at a steady pace. She gave Adnil a few instructions before giving the plane a voice command to take it off autopilot.

As Adnil held the control yoke, the plane felt steady and stable. "Are you sure it is not still on autopilot?"

"Yes, I am sure," said Katherine.

Adnil tested it by moving the control yoke a bit, causing the plane to tip slightly towards one side.

"Adnil, take it easy!" said Sky.

"Do you believe me now?" said Katherine.

"Yes, I do," said Adnil with a smile as she steadied the aircraft. A lot had happened since the days of enslavement, watching aircraft from the yard. Now she was a wild woman in flight, euphorically soaring through the sky. It felt powerful to be the one in the driver's seat of the aircraft, controlling its movements and finding freedom in the wind.

Adnil looked over her shoulder at Sky and their child in the back seat. Little Luna was sitting on Sky's lap, happy and content, like it was exactly where she belonged.

Hamish made goofy faces at the child, causing bouts of sweet musical laughter. The babe's eyes sparkled with delight as it waited excitedly in anticipation for the next goofy face to appear.

I can't wait for Joy to meet Luna. She was right all along, thought Adnil, remembering a conversation they had had in the compound. *One never knows what the future will bring. You can despair about the unfortunate fate you were dealt. But there could be a bright surreal future ahead of you, which is impossible to even imagine.*

Adnil looked out the front window into the vast expanse. She kept the aircraft steady as they moved forward smoothly. It had been a day of wonder and reclamation. She couldn't remember a time when she was happier—a thought that was becoming a regular occurrence. Just when she thought things couldn't get any better, they did.

Who knows what the future will bring. I am ready for it. I am a warrior—wild and free—and I am flying.

The End

Manufactured by Amazon.ca
Acheson, AB